Bello:

hidden talent rediscovered

Bello is a digital-only imprint of Pan Macmillan,
established to breathe new life into previously published,
classic books.

At Bello we believe in the timeless power of the imagination,
of a good story, narrative and entertainment, and we want to
use digital technology to ensure that many more readers
can enjoy these books into the future.

We publish in ebook and print-on-demand formats
to bring these wonderful books to new audiences.

www.panmacmillan.co.uk/bello

BELLO

Margaret Dickinson

Born in Gainsborough, Lincolnshire, Margaret Dickinson moved to the coast at the age of seven and so began her love for the sea and the Lincolnshire landscape.

Her ambition to be a writer began early and she had her first novel published at the age of twenty-seven. This was followed by twenty-seven further titles including *Plough the Furrow*, *Sow the Seed* and *Reap the Harvest*, which make up her Lincolnshire Fleethaven trilogy.

Many of her novels are set in the heart of her home county, but in *Tangled Threads* and *Twisted Strands* the stories include not only Lincolnshire but also the framework knitting and lace industries of Nottingham.

Her 2012 and 2013 novels, *Jenny's War* and *The Clippie Girls*, were both top twenty bestsellers and her 2014 novel, *Fairfield Hall*, went to number nine on the *Sunday Times* bestseller list.

Margaret Dickinson

ABBEYFORD
REMEMBERED

BELL◎

First published in 1999 by Severn House
Originally published 1981 under the title *Carrie*

This edition published 2014 by Bello
an imprint of Pan Macmillan Publishers Limited
Pan Macmillan, 20 New Wharf Road, London N1 9RR
Basingstoke and Oxford
Associated companies throughout the world

www.panmacmillan.co.uk/bello

ISBN 978-1-4472-9031-5 EPUB
ISBN 978-1-4472-9029-2 HB
ISBN 978-1-4472-9030-8 PB

Visit www.panmacmillan.com to read more about all our books
and to buy them. You will also find features, author interviews and
news of any author events, and you can sign up for e-newsletters
so that you're always first to hear about our new releases.

Author's Note

My writing career falls into two 'eras'. I had my first novel published at the age of twenty-five, and between 1968 and 1984 I had a total of nine novels published by Robert Hale Ltd. These were a mixture of light, historical romance, an action-suspense and one thriller, originally published under a pseudonym. Because of family commitments I then had a seven-year gap, but began writing again in the early nineties. Then occurred that little piece of luck that we all need at some time in our lives: I found a wonderful agent, Darley Anderson, and on his advice began to write saga fiction; stories with a strong woman as the main character and with a vivid and realistic background as the setting. Darley found me a happy home with Pan Macmillan, for whom I have now written twenty-one novels since 1994. Older, and with a maturity those seven 'fallow' years brought me, I recognize that I am now writing with greater depth and daring.

But I am by no means ashamed of those early works: they have been my early learning curve – and I am still learning! Originally, the first nine novels were published in hardback and subsequently in Large Print, but have never previously been issued in paperback or, of course, in ebook. So, I am thrilled that Macmillan, under their Bello imprint, has decided to reissue all nine titles.

Abbyeford, *Abbyeford Inheritance* and *Abbyeford Remembered* form a trilogy with a chequered history, which took four years to complete. It began life as a long, rambling 150,000 word novel, *Adelina*. On advice, this was cut drastically to about 60,000 words but it still failed to find a publisher. I started a sequel, *Carrie*, and this seemed to work much better. It was then suggested that this book should be submitted instead of *Adelina*, but to me that would have been wasting the first part of the story. I decided to put the two novels together and to write an earlier piece to start it all off, thereby forming one long novel again, but in three separate parts. This was then sent out to publishers and found acceptance. But – wait for it – the publishers wanted it split into three separate books. So, all three were published in 1981 by Robert Hale Ltd. as *Sarah*, *Adelina* and *Carrie*. At a later date, these were reissued by Severn House Publishers, again in hardback, under new titles and became *The Abbeyford Trilogy*.

Chapter One

Abbeyford, England, 1841

"What's this place called, then?"

Carrie Smithson stood at the top of the hill, looking down upon the village nestling in the valley below. The breeze blew her long black hair into a tangle of curls. Her arms akimbo, she stood with her feet, in their wooden clogs, planted slightly apart. Her thin blouse and coarse-woven skirt were flattened by the breeze against her young, firm body. She was slim, almost to the point of thinness, and yet there was a wiry strength about her and a determination about the set of her chin and in her eyes. It was her eyes which were her most striking feature. They were a most unusual colour – a deep violet.

She glanced towards her father standing beside her. His arms were folded across his broad chest. His eyes, as he gazed down into the valley, seemed far away, hazy with memories. He was small and stocky, yet immensely strong. He was dressed in a shirt with the sleeves rolled up above his elbows, a spotted neckcloth knotted carelessly about his throat. His feet were encased in boots with leather leggings buttoned each side as far as the knee. He wore breeches, worn and faded.

"I said, 'What's this place called', Pa?" Carrie prompted.

"Abbeyford."

"Are we going down?"

"I suppose so," he murmured.

"Why have we come here?"

"I've someone to see."

"Who? Someone you know? Have you been here before?"

"Aye. Twenty years ago 'n more, I lived here."

"Lived here?"

"I was born here."

"Really?" Eagerly her eyes scanned the valley. "Where? Which house?" She glanced at him and saw his gaze upon a square house just below them, standing halfway up the western hillside of the valley.

Innocently she asked, "Is that the house you were born in?"

Evan Smithson's laugh was more bitter than humorous. "Nay, child. The likes of us aren't born into Manor Houses. No," his eyes swivelled and dropped to the cottages nestling in the bottom of the valley. "*We're* born into hovels!"

"What about your parents? Are they still here?"

His eyes were on her, angry and resentful. Inwardly Carrie shrank a little but she gave no outward sign of fear and faced her father squarely.

"How the devil should I know?" he muttered. Carrie was shocked, but her questions ran on.

"Would you ever have come back, if it hadn't been for the railway coming this way?"

Carrie had never known any way of life other than the one they lived now. Her father – as far as she knew – had always been a ganger, the man in charge of the gangs of navvies building the new railways, his family moving after him wherever his work took him. As the railway lines extended slowly forward throughout the countryside, the Smithson family shifted once more, always moving a few miles in front of the line, living there until the line caught up with them and passed them by and then moving on once more. Home was a derelict cottage, a shack or even a farmer's barn. Sometimes their shelter was a mere tent of boughs and a tarpaulin, or a hastily constructed hut of stone and turf. Their possessions were few and loaded with monotonous regularity on to the pony and trap – their one means of removal.

"Aye, I'd have come back, some time, some day. I've unfinished business hereabouts."

"What?"

"You ask too many questions, girl," Evan growled and began to walk briskly down the hill towards the village. As she followed him Carrie's eyes still took in the scene before her. She pointed to the house she had imagined might have been her father's home. It was a square, solid house, with stables to one side and farm buildings to the rear.

"What's that place called, then?" Carrie asked, refusing to be cowed by his sharpness.

"Abbeyford Manor."

"Who lives there?"

"How should I know?" he replied testily, but she had the distinct feeling that he knew very well. That house had drawn his gaze and there had been a glint of bitterness in his eyes as he remembered – memories he had no intention of sharing with his daughter.

"What are those ruins? Right on top of the hill – above the Manor?"

"The abbey ruins. That's how the village gets its name. We're coming to the ford now."

The stream ran right across the lane down which they were walking towards the village. They crossed over by means of a small footbridge.

Carrie's restless eyes now turned to the eastern slope of the valley, where a half-timbered mansion – far grander than the Manor – stood just below the brow of the hill.

"What about that 'un? Who lives there?" Carrie's ceaseless curiosity continued.

"Abbeyford Grange. Used to be a Lord Royston live there. I 'spect he's dead now."

They were walking along the winding village street now. They passed the church in the centre of the village with the Vicarage close beside it and crossed the village green. Skirting the duck pond, they approached the line of small, squat cottages huddled around the green.

Carrie's sharp eyes darted about her. How quiet it seemed. How deserted almost. Many of the cottages were dilapidated. Broken windows were stuffed with sackcloth to keep out the cold and yet she could see that people still lived in them. Smoke curled from one or two chimneys and a scrawny black cat sprawled on a stone step, idly washing its face.

Evan stopped in front of one of the cottages facing the green and paused before reaching the door. This dwelling seemed in a better state of repair than the others. Bright flowers grew in the garden and pretty curtains blew at the windows. Carrie glanced back towards the next door cottage. Their window pane was broken, the remaining glass dirty and no curtains hung at the window. The garden was neglected and overgrown.

Evan knocked upon the door and Carrie stood on tiptoe, peering over his shoulder to see who would answer the door. When it opened, an old woman stood there, her eyes watering as she squinted up at them. Her hair was white and she stooped, her shoulders hunched, her thin, claw-like hand clasping her shawl about her.

"Who is it?" she asked in a quavering voice. "I can't see so well."

"Don't you know your own son, Mother?"

Carrie gasped to hear her father's tone of voice. There was no affection but a kind of belligerence in his words of greeting. The old woman's toothless mouth sagged open and she swayed slightly. Shading her eyes, she peered closely at him. "Evan? Is it – Evan?"

"Who else might it be? You have no other son, have you?"

A peculiar kind of choking sound escaped her thin lips. Again she seemed about to topple over. Carrie darted forward and caught hold of the woman's arm.

"Here, Grandmother, let me help you." She led the old lady back into the cottage and helped her to sit beside a blazing log fire. "There. We've given you a shock, coming unexpectedly like this."

She turned her brilliant eyes upon her father. "How can you be so unfeeling," she hissed at him, but Evan Smithson merely shrugged his shoulders and glanced about the cottage. "Been some changes here, I see."

Carrie, too, glanced around and then she jumped as she realised there was someone else in the tiny room. In a corner by the fire, sitting huddled in a chair, a rug over his knees was an old man.

His eyes glowered towards Evan and his thin hands, lined with purple veins, plucked restlessly at the rug on his knee.

"Well, well, well," Evan, too, had seen him and moved towards the old man. "You're still here then?"

"No thanks to you if I am. Crippled, I am, because of what you did ..."

"Hush, Henry," the old woman murmured worriedly.

"... Crippled ever since that night you led the whole village against the Trents, just because ..."

"No, Henry," her voice rose, shrill with fear, and his faded away to incoherent mutterings, and though Carrie strained to hear his words she could learn no more.

Evan's glance was still roving about the small room – the singing kettle on the hob, a rug covering the floor, two comfortable chairs and a blazing fire.

"Very cosy! Very comfortable!" Sarcasm lined his tone. "Put his hand in his pocket at last, did he?"

The old woman glanced at her son, her eyes pleading, her shrivelled mouth working but she uttered no sound. Evan's eyes, full of resentment, were upon his mother.

Intuitively, Carrie knew her father was not referring to Henry Smithson, huddled in the corner, a broken, pitiful figure. There was some mystery surrounding this household, events from the past which overshadowed the present and perhaps all their lives. She shuddered, and then to try to relieve the tense atmosphere, she said brightly, "I'm so happy to meet you, Grandma – and Grandpa, of course," she added hastily.

The old man's frown deepened and beneath his breath he still muttered darkly. Sarah Smithson tried, valiantly, to smile, but all the while her eyes, anxious and watchful, were upon her son.

"He's still alive, then?" Evan said.

Before his mother could answer, Henry Smithson's voice rose, more strongly, from the corner. "Aye, God rot his soul! Still up to his wicked ways – gambling and drunk most o' the time. Keeps selling land off to pay his debts."

Evan's interest sharpened visibly. He moved closer to the old man. "What d'you say? Selling land? How can he – he dunna own it?"

Henry Smithson sniggered. "A lot's happened since you left. That night – when you led the village men against the Trents – caused a lot of trouble and we've had to live with it ever since."

Evan brought his fist down upon the table with a thump. "We had every reason to rebel – the whole country was up in arms against the Corn Law. Remember Peterloo? How the magistrates called out the yeomanry to charge upon a peaceful meeting, killing and maiming innocent men, women and children?"

"Aye an' Wallis Trent did the same, didn't he? Called out the yeomanry against his own employees. Killed three and injured several – including me," Henry Smithson said bitterly. "I nearly died – wish to God I had. But I didn't, I've had to sit here the last twenty years – useless – and curse your name!"

Carrie gasped, shocked by the venom in the old man's tone. There was positive hatred in his attitude towards Evan, who, she believed, was his own son.

"Evan," Sarah's voice was hesitant, "did you know – Wallis Trent was killed that night?"

Evan turned sharply to look at his mother, surprise on his face. "No – no, I didn't. How? In the fire?"

"No – well, not exactly. He tried to rescue his horse from the burning stable," Sarah's eyes were downcast. "But the animal was wild with fear, reared and came down upon him, breaking his neck."

There was silence in the room whilst Carrie's eyes darted from one to another, trying to piece together the snippets of information she was hearing. She longed to ask for explanations but bit her lip to keep the ready questions in check.

Now was not the time.

"Adelina – what happened to his wife, Adelina?"

"She married Lord Lynwood."

Evan grinned suddenly. "Adelina – Lady Lynwood! Aye, an' it'll suit her, too."

Carrie's eyes widened. All these people her father seemed to know so well, she'd never heard of them, never heard him even speak of them. But then, she thought she had not even known before today that his own mother and father were still alive. She sat down on a low stool, resting her chin on her hands, her elbows on her knees and listened to their conversation, her sharp ears missing nothing, her violet eyes darting from one to another, but, for once, her tongue was still.

"What's this about *him* selling land?" her father was asking again.

"Lord Royston died and split his estate between Francesca, Adelina's daughter, and Jamie Trent. He left Abbeyford Grange and land to the north to her and the Manor and about five hundred acres to Jamie Trent," Henry explained.

"That was Wallis Trent's boy," Evan murmured.

"Squire Trent," Sarah spoke softly, "has control until Jamie reaches the age of twenty-five."

"And in the meantime," Henry added with malicious delight, "the old man has sold more than half of it off already!"

"Has he, b'God?" There was satisfaction in Evan's tone.

Within minutes Evan had taken his leave of his parents and hustled Carrie out of the door, scarcely giving her time to make her polite farewells. It was as if the sole purpose of his visit had been to find out about the Trents and having done so, he left.

He was striding up the village street towards the hill with Carrie taking little running steps to keep pace with him.

He seemed, now, a man with a purpose, as if the information he had learned had injected new life into his blood.

"Pa – Pa – what was all that about? What happened here? What was that about you and the villagers and the Trents? Pa ...?"

"Hold your tongue, girl. 'Tis none of your business."

Carrie fell silent, pouting her lips and wrinkling her nose moodily, but she knew better than to push her father or she would feel the weight of his hand.

Halfway up the hill, a horseman came galloping towards them. Drawing level, he reined in beside them. Carrie gazed up at the man on horseback towering above them. He was a young man of twenty or so, very tall and already broad-shouldered. His hair was dark brown with reddish highlights glinting in the sun. His face tanned and his eyes a deep brown, his chin was firm and resolute and his mouth set in a hard line. "Good-day."

Evan folded his arms across his chest and stood looking up at the young man. "Good-day – *sir*!" There was an unnecessary accent upon the salutation.

Carrie felt her pulses quicken as the young man's eyes strayed towards her. A slow smile touched his lips, softening their hardness, and his sombre expression lightened. "How do you do, Miss-er . . .?"

"Smithson. Carrie Smithson," she replied and smiled in return.

"I'm happy to meet you. My name is Jamie Trent."

Carrie's eyes widened and her lips parted in a gasp. She glanced swiftly at her father and saw that his eyes had narrowed calculatingly.

"I don't think I have seen you hereabouts before," Jamie Trent was saying, his eyes still upon Carrie's face. "Are you visiting?"

"My father is the . . ." Carrie had been about to say that her father was the ganger on the new railway, but Evan interrupted her. "We are visiting relatives, Mr Trent. Come, Carrie, it's time we were on our way."

His manner was curt, almost rude, and Carrie saw Jamie Trent's eyebrows rise fractionally and he glanced briefly towards her father, but it was Carrie to whom he spoke again. "I'll bid you good-day then, Miss Smithson. I hope we'll meet again."

Before she could utter a word, Jamie Trent had urged his horse forward and was soon cantering down the hill away from them. Carrie's violet eyes followed him.

"Come along, girl," Evan said roughly. Reluctantly Carrie turned and followed her father, but all the way up the hill she kept glancing back towards the now tiny figure of the young man on horseback.

Some three miles to the north of Abbeyford, at the top of a rise, they stopped to look down at the workings of the railway below. Like an open wound, the railway gouged its way through farmland, woodland, rock, over water, even through hillsides. The gang of navvies over whom Evan Smithson was the ganger, scurried about like a colony of working ants. As they neared the site, Carrie could see the men, some stripped to the waist under the hot summer sun, shovelling the earth and rocks into the carts which, when loaded, were pulled away by horses, five hundred or so men and over one hundred and fifty horses, working over a three-mile stretch. Like their ganger, they found shelter wherever they could – in empty village cottages, in barns, sleeping two or three to a makeshift bed, some even with their wives and families sharing the harsh life. They worked hard and yet throughout the country the navvies had a bad reputation for causing havoc wherever they appeared. Not only did the railway itself meet with opposition from the country dwellers as it tore its way through their lands and their livelihood, but the arrival of five hundred hard-drinking, swearing navvies in a peaceful village was something to be feared.

Only the contractor's men who held a position of some importance – the engineer, the engine drivers, the foreman and skilled men – could find comfortable accommodation in the village. For the rest, the labouring navvies, it meant finding a bed wherever they could.

Yet there was a strange camaraderie amongst these ruffians, built like an army of Goliaths. They ate meat in huge amounts and consumed vast quantities of ale. They fought and gambled and yet they worked hard – exceedingly hard – with great courage, seeming to have a contemptuous disregard for even the most dangerous work. Whilst they appeared to have little respect for the various communities upon which they descended, there was loyalty amongst themselves and when any of their number suffered fatal injury, his brother-navvies would suddenly become a group of silent mourners at the nearest church.

"I'll be off home, now," Carrie said. She did not want to go too near the workmen. Not that she was afraid of them, for Caroline Smithson feared no one, not even her swift-tempered father, but the men's whistles and calls caused her an embarrassment she would sooner avoid. More than once she had had to skip smartly aside to avoid their reaching hands and once, when a hulking brute had managed to lay hold of her she had had to fight, claw and scratch her way free of his loathsome embrace. She admired the tenacity and pluck of the navvies as workmen, but she had no desire to lead this life for ever. There must be a better life than this, Carrie told herself, somewhere, somehow, and so she kept a safe distance from the lusty navvies.

"Make yourself presentable, girl," her father said. "Lloyd Foster will be calling. Brush your hair – you look like a gypsy!"

"Ain't surprising," Carrie retorted boldly, "since we live like gypsies." She began to run down the hill out of reach of her father's hand as he raised it to cuff her. His eyes glittered with momentary anger and then he laughed aloud, the breeze carrying the sound to the ears of the running girl so that she turned, grinned cheekily at him, waved briefly and then ran on. Of all his family, only Carrie dared to oppose her father or speak her mind and only she could do so and escape his vicious temper.

Nearing the shack which was the Smithsons' present dwelling-place, Carrie slowed her pace.

Lloyd Foster! She wrinkled her nose and her generous mouth pouted. She could see his horse tethered outside the shack and knew he was waiting for her.

Lloyd Foster was an important man – he was the Boss. He was the man who held the contract for the building of the railway and yet he was still a young man. He was a flamboyant character, loud, brash, even vulgar and yet likeable. At least, most people liked him, responding readily to his never-failing good humour, his happy-go-lucky manner. All except Carrie. Even though she knew Lloyd Foster wanted her, she refused to let herself like him.

Carrie peeped through the small, grimy window. She could see her mother sitting at the bare, scrubbed table, her elbows on the table, her hands cupped to hold her weary head. Her knuckles were misshapen, swollen and painful with the rheumatism which afflicted the whole of her body. She was looking towards the man who stood in front of the makeshift fireplace – Lloyd Foster. He was tall with dark, tanned skin, fair, curling hair, bright blue eyes and a wide and ever-laughing mouth. He was standing, tall and straight, his chest thrown out, rocking backwards and forwards slightly on his heels, his thumbs stuck into the armholes of his gaudy waistcoat. A thick cigar was clamped between his white, even teeth. His clothes were always of the finest material. His shirt was sparkling white and his riding-coat and breeches well cut. His black leather boots shone and always there was a gold watch chain looped across his broad chest.

Carrie sighed and pushed open the door. Lloyd Foster turned at once and made an exaggerated bow towards her, then spoilt the courtly gesture by smacking her on the backside as she passed close to him.

"I'll thank you to keep your hands to yourself, Mr Foster."

Lloyd Foster's loud laugh threatened to bring the dilapidated shack tumbling down about them. But Carrie merely glanced at him and moved out of reach again as he made to put his arm about her waist.

"Ah, Miss Carrie, an' don't I be lovin' you the more when you're angry." His rich Irish brogue mocked her good-humouredly. It was impossible to offend the man, Carrie thought, and in spite of herself she found the corners of her mouth twitching into the beginnings of a smile. It was very difficult to maintain a mood of anger with him when all he did was laugh and tease and pay extravagant compliments.

Lloyd Foster was something of an enigma. No one knew anything about his background, only that he was a railway builder – one of the best in the country and he was a clever man with people, Carrie thought. The gangs of navvies who worked on the western railways were often made up largely of Irish and to hear their own delightful brogue from the lips of the Boss himself ensured hard work and loyalty from them. The railway site rang with his boisterous laughter and the workmen's faces, glistening with sweat, would break into a grin at the sight of the tall man on his horse. Also, he was reputedly generous to a fault towards his employees, so much so that other contractors on rival lines grumbled that he attracted all their best navvies into his gangs!

"I'm supposed to be here on a matter of business wid your

father, me darlin', but 'tis all a devious plot, for me eyes were hungry for sight of your lovely face."

Carrie raised her eyebrows cynically and glanced at her mother.

Lucy Smithson sat at the table, leaning wearily against it, her eyes dark pools of suffering and bitterness. The years of itinerant living had treated her harshly. Her once black hair was now grey and dull. Her body was thin and shapeless, her hands wrinkled and work-worn. Lucy had borne seven children of whom only four now survived. The others were buried in different parishes, their unmarked graves in churchyards alongside the railway line. One had died of typhoid and two of consumption. And now Luke, Lucy's first-born, suffered from that same terrible cough. The two younger children, Tom and Matthew, only fourteen and thirteen, yet already working on the railway bed, were sickly too. Of all Lucy's children only Carrie, now aged eighteen, was healthy, strong and resilient. And of all of them only Carrie was not afraid of Evan.

"Will ye be takin' a walk wid me, Miss Carrie?" Lloyd Foster was saying, bending towards her. Carrie opened her mouth to refuse but at that moment the door opened and Evan Smithson came in.

"Ah, an' now here's the man himself," Lloyd Foster said. "An' how is me darlin' railway comin' along under your guiding hand, Mr Smithson?"

Evan grinned and slapped Lloyd Foster on the back, for, although in theory, Lloyd Foster was his employer, in practice Evan enjoyed an unusual position of equality with him. Such was the amiability of Lloyd Foster that no one, not even the youngest navvy with the most menial task, was ever made to feel his inferior. He made each and every one of them feel that all of them together were building the railway.

Evan turned towards his wife and daughter, his face once more hard. He jerked his thumb in the direction of the door.

"Out – we've business to discuss."

Tiredly, Lucy levered herself and moved, without argument, towards the door, but Carrie, hands on hips, faced her father squarely. "Why? What's so secret?"

"None of your business, me girl. Get!"

"Ah, sure an' me lovely lass can stay if she'll sit an' hold me hand."

"Not *this* time," Evan said firmly. "We've men's affairs to talk on." He glanced meaningly at Foster, who shrugged, laughed, and slapping Carrie once more on the backside said, "Now don't you be goin' too far away, me girl."

Carrie moved towards the door of the shack. To her left hung an old brown curtain, dividing the small area where her parents slept from the rest of the shack. Carrie opened the door and then glanced back towards the two men. She was curious to know what lay behind her father's secretiveness. Their backs were towards her so she shut the door with a slam, as if she had left the shack, but instead she slipped stealthily behind the curtain. Her heart was beating rapidly as she sat quietly on the shakedown on the floor and pulled the worn blanket over her. Silent, she sat listening to the voices of the men, her father's sometimes low so that she had to strain to hear his words, but Lloyd Foster she could hear plainly.

"And what did ye find out then, me friend?" Foster was saying. She heard the rustle of paper and could only guess that her father was unfolding a map. She had seen them use one before to plan the route of the railway line.

"It's even better than I had hoped," Evan replied, and there was a kind of suppressed excitement in his tone. "The best route is right across the land which now belongs to the Trents. And Squire Guy Trent's tight for money. Drinks and gambles all his grandson's inheritance away. He's ripe, I tell you!" There was a dull thud as if Evan had thumped the table with his fist in his enthusiasm.

"Gambles, is it, you say? Ah, a man after me own heart! And where is it you think our railway should run?"

Again Carrie heard the rustle of paper and imagined their heads bent together over the map as she had seen them so many times. She heard her father's voice. "We continue south from where we are now, making a cutting through this small incline, then into Abbeyford valley, between the hills to the east and west. We'll need an embankment, but the best line would be between the Manor

House and the stream and continue south out of the valley. We can get through the dip between these two lines of hills quite easily."

"Mmm," Lloyd Foster's tone was, for once, serious – the only time he was ever serious was when discussing his beloved railway. "I'll be needin' to survey the whole district. 'Tis me engineer's job by rights, but you know when 'tis me own livelihood I'm gamblin' I like to be seein' the cards for meself."

Carrie knew that, although a fine engineer by the name of Thomas Quincy, who also happened to be a surveyor, was employed on this line, Foster himself always surveyed the land and knew the workings of the line as well as any engineer. And she also knew that the money which built the railway was not his own but that of the Railway Board – men who invested capital into such schemes with the hope of becoming even richer than they already were.

There was a pause, then Foster added, "What about skirting these hills – avoidin' Abbeyford all together?"

"No!" Evan's tone was sharp. "To the east there's more hills and if you veer to the west you'll go through Lynwood's lands – not the Trents!"

"And will that be mattering?"

"Well – he'll demand a higher way-leave for his land. I reckon we'd be better to buy off a good deal of Trent's land – we ought to have a station or a halt hereabouts, anyway."

"Aye, maybe you're right as ever, me boy." Foster's ready laugh rang out. "You'll be takin' me job if I don't watch out. Tell me now, what is it about these Trents? Your face seems to change when you speak of them and you're determined the railroad shall run through their land, are ye not?"

"It's none of your concern," Evan growled.

Behind the curtain Carrie stifled a gasp. Despite Lloyd Foster's friendliness, he was still Evan's employer and she had never heard her father be deliberately rude to him before. But, even now, Foster took no offence. Reluctantly, Evan added, "I've an old score to settle. By rights, the Manor House should be mine!"

"Yours? How?" Foster's tone registered surprise, but that was nothing to the astonishment Carrie, in her hiding-place, felt.

"It's a long story," Evan muttered, his voice now so low that Carrie could scarcely hear. "Just take my word for it. I aim to ruin the Trents and live there mesel' – one day!"

"Well, now, me boy," Foster's hearty laugh rang out. "I just might be able to help you there. I have plans of me own, don't you know, and there's something *I* want – very much – that maybe *you* could be helpin' *me*."

"What's that?"

"Ah, now never mind for de moment. Maybe in time we'll both be gettin' what we want."

"Hmm, mebbe." Evan sounded doubtful. There was the rustle of paper again as he refolded the map. "Shall we go and have a look at the land?" It sounded as if Evan were trying to change the subject now. Carrie heard him move towards the door and the curtain shook. She froze, holding her breath, fearful her father would come behind the curtain and discover she had been eavesdropping.

Carrie heard the door slam and their footsteps move away from the shack and she breathed again. She waited some moments before moving from her cramped position till she was sure they had really gone. She thought about her father's bitter words. 'The Manor House should be mine . . . I'll ruin the Trents and live there mesel'.'

The picture of Jamie Trent, the tall, handsome young man on horseback she had met but once, came before her mind's eye and inexplicably her heart began to beat a little faster at the thought of him.

Chapter Two

Two days later, in the early afternoon, Carrie slipped away from the shack and, avoiding the railway workings, made her way across the fields and up the hill towards Abbeyford. She was determined to get to know her grandmother better, yet she had had the intuitive sense to keep her intentions secret.

Carrie tapped at the cottage door with some trepidation, remembering the unwelcoming figure of the hunched cripple in the corner – her grandfather, and yet he seemed to bear such hatred for his son, Evan.

The door opened and Sarah Smithson's wrinkled face lit up with pleasure at the unexpected visit from her granddaughter. "Come in, my dear, come in."

Carrie followed her slow-moving steps into the small back scullery where they could talk freely without the malevolent presence of Henry Smithson's scowling face.

"Tell me about yourself, child." Her old eyes roved over the girl's lovely face, as if she would draw strength from Carrie's youthful vitality.

Carrie shrugged and smiled. "There's not much to tell. There were seven of us children, but three died in childhood. There's Luke – he's twenty, the oldest." A shadow flickered across her violet eyes, "but he's not strong. Then there's mesel' – I'm eighteen. Then there's Tom and Matthew – they're fourteen and thirteen. They all work on the railway – with Pa. I help Ma as best I can." She broke off and asked, "Do you know me Ma?"

"I might. Is her name Lucy?"

Carrie nodded.

Sarah Smithson sighed. "Yes, I thought so. Lucy Walters. She disappeared when Evan first left Abbeyford."

Carrie leant forward eagerly. "Grandma – will you tell me about me Pa? What caused him to leave home . . .?"

"No, no," the old woman cried sharply. "I cannot speak of it! He – he is not welcome here. People remember. He should not have come back." Her words were halting and painful to her, Carrie could see. She bit back the words of pleading which sprang to her lips. She could not cause her grandmother more pain by making her relive unpleasant memories, but she longed to learn the truth.

Some time later Carrie took her leave. The summer sun was warm upon her head, and in the quiet of the valley she felt a peace settle upon her. She wandered along the lane, reluctant to return to the shack she must call home. Her gaze roamed the hills on either side. The mansion to the east called Abbeyford Grange and then opposite the Manor House and above it, silhouetted sharply against the blue sky, gaunt and lonely, stood the abbey ruins. Intrigued to see them, Carrie took the lane leading towards Abbeyford Manor. As she drew level with the house she looked at it with interest. This was where Jamie Trent lived – and it was the house her father coveted. He had vowed to bring ruin to the Trent family because of some deep ill-will he bore them, some revenge he sought. His reasons, buried deep in the past, were a mystery to his daughter.

Even in the warm afternoon sun Carrie shivered, and moved on up the lane past the gate leading to the Manor's stables and on up the hill towards the wood.

Beneath the trees it was cooler and shady and quiet save for the sounds of the woodland creatures. She took off her heavy clogs and delighted in the feel of the long grass on her bare feet. Joyously she skipped along, light-hearted and for once free from the cares of her harsh life.

As she emerged from the wood she stood a moment looking down on the valley below, her eyes tracing the line her father had suggested to Lloyd Foster that their railway should follow, entering the valley from the north and running alongside the stream directly in front of the Manor and on southwards to the natural pass out of the valley.

"Why," she spoke aloud in surprise, "the line will cut right through his pastures – and his cornfields!" She remembered her father's bitter words, 'I'll ruin the Trents', and she frowned thoughtfully. Perhaps he had planned the route to come through the Trents' land intentionally for the very purpose of ruining them.

She shaded her eyes against the sun. Carrie expected to see men working in the fields, but there seemed a strange lack in numbers. Certainly there were one or two tiny figures in the far distance, moving about their work in the fields. She saw a horseman cantering along the side of the stream and then turn up the hill towards her. As he drew closer she saw the rider was Jamie Trent. He reined in beside her and sat, tall and straight, upon his horse. He wore breeches and knee-boots and an open-necked shirt. His brow glistened with sweat and his shirt was stained darkly with the signs of hard labour.

Why, thought Carrie in surprise, he's been working in the fields alongside his labourers.

He was smiling down at her. "Miss Smithson. How good it is to see you again." His voice was warm and deep, and Carrie's heart beat a little faster.

"Mr Trent," she murmured, almost shyly, though her eyes regarded him boldly, taking in every detail of his dark, handsome face, his deep brown eyes and rugged jaw line. He dismounted and stood beside her, the manly closeness of him quickening her pulses.

"I hoped we might meet again, but I had no idea where you came from – or why you came visiting Abbeyford."

"I – we – came to visit my grandmother, Mrs Smithson."

Jamie Trent's eyebrows rose a fraction. "Oh! I had no idea she had any children, let alone a granddaughter. Where do you live?"

"I – er . . ." Carrie hesitated. Now she wanted to keep the fact that she was linked with the railway a secret from Jamie Trent. He could not welcome the railway which threatened the Trent farmlands – nor the people who built it! "We're staying, just temporary, over the hills there." She waved her hand vaguely in a northerly direction.

"May I escort you home? It's a long way and my horse will carry the two of us easily."

Carrie drew breath sharply, torn between the desire to remain in his company, close beside him on horseback and the wish to keep her identity a secret.

"I'd – be very glad of a ride, Mr Trent, but I don't like to trouble you . . ."

"It's no trouble, Miss Smithson." His voice was low and his eyes were upon her face. "It will be my pleasure."

He lifted her easily on to his brown mare and mounted behind her. His arm circled her waist lightly, her shoulder was warm against his chest and she could feel his breath on her cheek. The horse moved on at walking pace, down the hill and then following the winding path of the stream. Carrie, acutely aware of the whole time of his closeness, glanced up towards the Manor House – his home – as they passed before it.

"That's where you live, ain't it? It's a lovely house."

When he didn't answer at once, she glanced up at him, her eyes only inches from his face.

"It – could be," he said guardedly, offering no further explanation. Carrie bit back the questions on her lips, sensing that she could not probe into his life. Glancing again at the square, solid Manor House, she saw now that on closer inspection there was an air of neglect about it. The windows were dull, the paint peeling. The garden was overgrown with long grass and weeds. She didn't know what to say, so they rode in silence until Abbeyford was far behind them. Then Jamie Trent seemed to relax. He smiled down at her. "Are we taking the right direction? You still haven't told me where it is you're staying."

"Oh – er – about two miles further on. Are those fields yours?"

Again the frown was fleetingly across his handsome face. "Yes, and I'll see they stay that way."

Carrie's heart pounded. The railway! She guessed he referred to the railway trying to encroach upon his lands. But his brown eyes were looking down into her face, quite unaware that she belonged to the railway people.

"Tell me about yourself, Miss Smithson – Carrie, isn't it?"

She nodded. "There's not much to tell," her voice was husky. What could she tell him? Of her family's gypsy existence? Of their harsh way of life? About her father? No, no, she couldn't mention him – or the railway! And yet, that *was* her life!

He was smiling, interpreting her reticence as natural shyness. "Oh I'm sure that's not so. You're – you're a very pretty girl."

She smiled a little shyly – she was unused to such gentle compliments.

"Please – tell me about your family?" she asked softly. Again his face darkened, but because it would be churlish to ignore such a direct request, he said slowly, "My parents are dead. So, too, is my grandmother – my father's mother. My own mother died giving birth to me. Now there's only my grandfather, Squire Guy Trent and myself."

"Oh, but I thought your mother . . ." Carrie stopped, shocked that she had allowed her chattering tongue to slip.

"What?"

"No matter – please go on." But now her mind was in a turmoil.

"My father was killed in 1819 when I was only small."

"How – did it happen?" Her heart beat fast. She was almost afraid to hear his answer and yet she had to ask, she had to know.

"Oh, there was much unrest amongst the workers at that time, so my grandfather says, and one man who seemed to have a vendetta against the Trents led the villagers in revolt."

Carrie was not sure what the word 'vendetta' meant, but she could guess! Now she was silent.

"They threatened to march upon the Manor if my father did not give them better wages."

"And – and did they?" she asked faintly.

"Aye," Jamie Trent answered grimly. "But my father had been forewarned of this. My stepmother and my grandfather had, whilst out riding, come across a secret meeting of the village men in the abbey ruins. My father called out the yeomanry and as the village men marched upon the Manor the soldiers galloped down upon them."

A vivid picture of the crippled old man – her own grandfather, she believed – flashed before her eyes. So that was how Henry Smithson had been maimed. And the revolt had been led by Evan Smithson, her own father. *He* was the man of whom Jamie spoke as having a – a vendetta against the Trent family. She frowned, vaguely remembering something else. It had been when her grandmother had been telling Evan that Wallis Trent – Jamie's father – had been killed that night. Now, what was it her father had said . . .?

"Was there a fire at the Manor?" she turned her violet eyes towards Jamie. His face only a breath away, his lips so close to her hair.

"Why, yes," there was surprise in his tone. "How did you know?"

"Oh – I – er – well," Carrie was flustered. There she went again, letting her curiosity outrun her. Why, why, did she not think before she spoke? "You said – you said they were marching on the Manor – I suppose they meant to do it damage – and fire . . ."

"Yes," Jamie agreed. "One of them – the leader – escaped, mainly, I believe, because my stepmother went to warn the villagers."

"Your stepmother?" Now it was Carrie's turn to show surprise.

"Yes. She did not agree with my father that the yeomanry should be called out. She tried to prevent the bloodshed."

"How very brave of her." Carrie said swiftly, and then once more regretted her hasty words. Perhaps Jamie had believed his father to be in the right.

"Or foolhardy – whichever way you like to look at it." His tone, gave nothing away.

"And – which way do you look at it?" she asked boldly.

She felt the sigh rise in his chest and then upon her hair. "I cannot judge. There was much bitterness. I understand my father was a hard man – hated by the villagers. Perhaps there was cause – I don't know. He was trying to rescue his favourite stallion from the burning stables. The animal was wild and killed him."

Carrie remembered now – that was what her grandmother, Sarah Smithson, had said.

"And your stepmother?"

Jamie smiled and there was a gentleness in his eyes. "She's Lady Adelina Lynwood now. She's very beautiful and has always been very kind to me. I'm very fond of her."

Adelina! Her father had spoken of her as if he had known her. But so he might have done, for she had been Wallis Trent's second wife and therefore mistress of the Manor for a while.

Now it was Jamie's turn to ask probing questions. "Your grandparents are Sarah and Henry Smithson?"

"Y-yes," Carrie answered guardedly, her heart beating fast again.

"Strange," Jamie murmured. "I had not heard of their son. He must have left home many years ago."

"I don't know," the words came out in a rush. "I didn't even know he came from hereabouts until the other day."

"Really? Has he never talked about his family or . . .?"

"You can put me down now, Mr Trent, I can walk the rest of the way. It's only over the next hill."

"Oh, please allow me to take you . . ."

"No, no," Carrie said, wriggling a little as if to slide from the horse. "Me Pa, if he sees me with you, he'll like as not beat me."

"Oh, I see." Suddenly Jamie grinned making his usually serious face seem boyish and mischievous. "I wouldn't like that!"

"Nor would I!" Carrie retorted with feeling and grinned back at him. Their shared secret meeting seemed to bring them close.

He dismounted and held up his arms towards her and she slid from the horse's back into them. He did not release her immediately but stood looking down at her.

"Carrie – oh Carrie," his voice was suddenly husky. "You've the loveliest eyes I've ever seen . . ."

Without warning his arms were strong iron bands about her and his mouth was hot upon hers. Readily Carrie responded to his kisses, her heart pounding fiercely. At last they drew apart, their eyes shining, their hot breath mingling, startled by the suddenness, the newness of this emotion.

"I'll – see you again?" he whispered.

Carrie, innocent of all guile, nodded, her mind in a turmoil. Hastily, suddenly afraid they'd be seen, she broke away from him and ran up the hill.

"Tomorrow?" he called after her. She paused in her flight, turned and waved. He returned her wave and then she was running up the hill again, her feet hardly touching the ground, her heart singing. At the top she turned. He was sitting astride his horse now, but still watching her.

He waved again and she lifted her hand in farewell, then Jamie turned his horse and cantered back towards Abbeyford.

When he was a small speck in the distance, Carrie turned and began to walk slowly down the other side of the hill towards the railway workings.

Carrie's mood of joy was short-lived. As she neared the bank overlooking the railway workings she saw her three brothers climbing towards her.

Luke, the eldest, was in the centre, leaning heavily upon the two younger boys, who themselves looked scarcely to have the strength to help him. All three were thin, their clothes ragged and they were covered – clothes, skin and hair – in the grey dust from the stone they had hewn since early morning. It was early for them to be coming home, and Carrie ran to them in alarm, fearful that Luke must have been hurt in some accident.

"What is it? What's the matter?" she cried anxiously, swiftly taking the place of Tom at Luke's side.

" 'Ee's bin coughin' 'is guts up!" volunteered Matt, and as Carrie searched the thin, sickly face of her elder brother, her heart gave a lurch. There was a thin trickle of blood at the corner of his mouth. She'd seen that before. One of the other children, who had died of consumption a year back, had coughed up blood!

"Dunna let on to Pa," Luke gasped, "that we've come away 'aforetime."

" 'Course I won't," Carrie replied with affectionate impatience and gave his shoulder a squeeze. "What d'you take me for?"

As they neared the shack, a handsome gig pulled by a high-stepping pony and carrying two women came lurching down the cart-track towards them. The older woman, holding the reins, pulled the pony to a halt beside Carrie and her brothers. Carrie stared open-mouthed at the two women – ladies without doubt. She had never seen such finery – silk dresses and bonnets, with delicate lace trimmings. The older one, whom she presumed to be the younger girl's mother, was still a beautiful woman, with smooth skin, green eyes and lovely auburn hair arranged to frame her face. The younger girl, too, was undoubtedly pretty but there was a discontented pout to her mouth and a coldness in her blue eyes. She twirled the parasol she held and sighed with boredom. The older lady was returning Carrie's gaze with equal interest, almost as if she half-recognised the girl and yet could not recollect where or when she had seen her before. But Carrie was quite certain that she had never before seen this lovely lady – she would not have forgotten!

"Are you belonging the railway?" the lady asked, her voice low and sweet with a slightly strange accent. American, Carrie thought, for she remembered a Yankee who'd worked as a navvy for a time had spoken the same way.

"Yes, ma'am." The courtesy came naturally to her lips. "Me Pa's the ganger."

The lady's eyes were puzzled.

"He's in charge o' the navvies – workmen, ma'am," Carrie explained.

"Oh, I see. Then is he the man who plans the way the railway should go?"

"Not really. That's the contractor or the engineer an' surveyor."

"Then I guess it's one of them I want to see. Could you tell me where I might find them?"

"Well . . ." Carrie hesitated and glanced at Luke.

Her brother's eyes were fixed, mesmerised, upon the young girl sitting beside her mother in the gig.

"Luke, do you know where Lloyd Foster might be?"

Luke did not answer. Carrie prodded him gently. "Luke . . .?"

He jumped. "What?"

"I said do you know where Lloyd Foster is?"

Luke, his eyes still fixed upon the girl, said, "I dunno – oh, down near the bed, I think."

"That's the railway workings, ma'am," Carrie said.

"Thank you, I . . ."

At that moment there was a rattle behind them and the shack door flew open.

"What the devil . . .?" As Carrie heard her father's voice raised in anger, she saw the lady's eyes move from Carrie's face to look beyond her. The lovely woman's green eyes widened and her lips parted in a shocked gasp. Her face turned pale. She must have pulled, involuntarily, upon the reins, for suddenly the pony whinnied and shied, tipping the little gig dangerously. The young girl gave a delicate shriek of alarm whilst her mother fought to control not only the animal but also her own runaway emotions.

Carrie felt Luke shake off her supporting arm and move forward to help, but already Evan Smithson had moved swiftly and calmly to the horse's head and Luke's gangling figure stood uselessly by, his gaze once more returning to the girl's face.

Evan, stroking the horse's nose, grinned up at the woman in the gig. Carrie watched, fascinated.

"You!" the woman breathed. Words seemed to desert her, for she just said again, as if she could not believe it, "*You!*"

"Aye, m'lady. It's me." Then, almost insolently, he added, "I'm gratified you ain't forgotten me."

The colour was returning to her face. "As if I could!" she muttered bitterly. Then her glance rested briefly upon Carrie and her brothers. "Are these your – children?"

Evan nodded. "I married Lucy – you remember her?"

"I do."

Evan's grin widened and he laughed aloud. "She's changed – you'd scarce recognise her now."

"I don't doubt life with you has altered her," the lady said wryly. Then she nodded towards Carrie. "But she has the look of her grandmother – Sarah."

Evan's eyes hardened with bitterness.

"So," the lady was saying thoughtfully, "you're a railway builder now, are you?"

"Yes, my lovely lady, I am."

"And where – exactly – might your railway be going?"

Evan's eyes glinted. "You've naught to fear, m'lady. 'T will not cross your land."

A small sigh escaped the beautiful woman's lips and she said flatly, with what Carrie thought to be exceptional insight, "Across the Trents' land, I suppose?"

Then Carrie realised the lady was not merely guessing. This lovely woman knew her pa, and her ma and grandma, and knew, too, that Evan was planning to cross the Trents' land with his railway, and the tone of her voice told Carrie that she knew, too, the reasons behind his plan. She knew why he planned to ruin the Trents!

"Can't you leave them alone? Haven't you had enough revenge – even yet?" she asked Evan in a low voice.

Slowly Evan shook his head, his mouth set.

"Then I'll bid you good-day, Mr Smithson." She slapped the pony with the reins at the same moment Evan let go of the animal's head.

"Good-day, my lovely Adelina," Evan murmured softly, more to himself, for the gig was already bouncing away from them over the rough track. His eyes followed its progress.

"Pa?" Luke and Carrie spoke together. "Who was that?" "Who are they?"

For a moment Evan did not answer, his eyes still upon the disappearing vehicle.

"Lady Adelina Lynwood."

Carrie gasped. So that was Jamie Trent's stepmother.

"And the girl? Who was the lovely girl?" Luke, with unusual boldness, persisted, his eyes too following the two women.

Evan shrugged. "Her daughter, I suppose."

Luke, still gazing up the track, began to cough, his thin body shaking. The sound seemed to break Evan's reverie. "What you doin' home so early, eh?" he asked roughly.

" 'T was Luke," Matt piped up. " 'Ee's sick."

"Sick?" Evan scoffed. "We've no time to be sick, boy. We've a railway to build!"

Carrie flared angrily. "Don't be so heartless, Pa. Can't you *see* he's ill – like – like . . ." She bit her tongue and glanced hastily at Luke, but he was oblivious to them all, his gaze even yet straining for sight of the gig, even though moments before it had dropped down a slope and disappeared from view.

"Ill – me foot!" Evan gave a click of exasperation, and his resentful gaze included not only Luke but his two younger sons also. "Why she can only bear me wreckling sons, I dunnot know." Then his eyes rested upon Carrie. "Still, there's you, me lass, ain't there." He pinched her cheek with a rough gesture which was the closest Evan Smithson would ever come to a sign of affection. "Mebbe *you'll* be the one to help me get what I want, eh?"

Without further explanation Evan strode away, his strange words bringing an inexplicable chill to his daughter's heart.

The following day Carrie was unable to slip away over the hill to Abbeyford to meet Jamie Trent. Luke stayed in the shack, too ill to drag himself to the railway site, and Carrie, whilst wanting to nurse her brother, chafed inwardly at her enforced captivity. She was unusually impatient with him, fretting for fear Jamie would misinterpret her absence and would think that she no longer wished to meet him, when in truth her heart yearned for sight of him.

Luke lay on the straw shakedown with only an old coat as a cover and stared at the rough boards of the roof, his thoughts far away from the harsh surroundings. Carrie had a shrewd idea what – or rather who – filled his thoughts and this was confirmed when Luke said pensively, "I don't think I've ever seen such a beautiful girl."

Carrie sniffed derisively. "Huh! Anyone can be beautiful if they're rich. She looked right uppity to me."

Luke raised himself on his elbow. "How can you judge when you dunna know her?"

"Then how can *you* judge?" she retorted sharply.

"I . . ." But whatever he had been going to say was cut off by an attack of coughing, after which he lay back exhausted.

"There, you see, you go upsetting yourself and making yourself worse."

"I just wanted to know – who she is – that's all," Luke said weakly.

"Yes – yes, all right," Carrie soothed, contrite now that her arguing with him had brought on a coughing fit. "I'll – see if I can find out more about her, but try to rest now."

Luke closed his eyes and slept.

So it was three days before Carrie's flying feet took her over the hills once more to Abbeyford.

As she topped the hill overlooking the village she scanned the fields anxiously for sight of Jamie – but she could not see him. Then she was running pell-mell down the hill towards the squat cottages where her grandparents lived. She had decided to visit her grandma each time she came to see Jamie, thereby establishing some kind of alibi for herself should her Pa ever hear of her visits to Abbeyford and question her.

The old woman's eyes glowed as she saw Carrie again. "My dear child, come away in!"

After she had spent a pleasant half-hour chatting with the old lady in the kitchen of the small cottage Carrie grew restless, anxious to be off now in search of Jamie. Then she remembered her promise to Luke.

"Grandma, a fine carriage came by the railway the other day. Pa said it was Lady Adelina Lynwood."

The pleasure died on Sarah Smithson's face, her eyes were suddenly once again wary and pain-filled and her shrunken lips trembled. "Oh – was it?" she murmured guardedly, now avoiding her granddaughter's eyes when moments before she had gazed fondly into Carrie's face.

"Yes. There was a young girl with her – a year or two older than me, I should think. Who would she be, Grandma?"

Sarah sighed heavily, then said. "I suppose it would be her daughter, Francesca."

"Oh, is she a Trent, then?" Carrie asked, interested in anyone who might be connected with Jamie.

After a moment's hesitation, Sarah said flatly, "No – she's Lynwood's daughter. I – used to be quite friendly with Adelina – Lady Lynwood – once. She came from America and had a daughter by Lord Lynwood before she was married."

Carrie gasped, but listened.

"Then she left Lynwood. They quarrelled – and she married Wallis Trent. But it was not a happy marriage. He was a hard, cold man who treated his employees – and I guess his wife too – as possessions and bent everyone to his will." She sighed as she remembered. "Then there was unrest amongst the farm workers."

Carrie nodded, compressing her lips. "Led by Pa?"

Sarah glanced fearfully at her but was obliged to nod agreement.

"Then I suppose," Carrie continued, guessing the end of the story before Sarah had finished the telling of it. "When Wallis Trent was killed, she was reunited with Lord Lynwood. How romantic!"

Sarah murmured bitterly, "Romantic, you call it, eh? Real life is not at all romantic. It's cruel and harsh and ..." She stopped, startled at herself for unleashing her own emotions which had been stifled for many years. "I've said too much," she muttered roughly. "It's time you were going, girl."

Surprised by her grandmother's swift change of mood, Carrie left. She had found out what she wanted to know and now she wanted to meet Jamie. She took the lane towards the Manor House, but the only sounds were the twittering of the birds in the hedgerows and the rustling of the creatures in the long grass. The sun was hot on her head and her bare feet became covered with the dry dust from the lane. She drew level with the Manor House and stood at the gate leading into the stableyard. Everywhere was still and silent – no sign of activity in the yard, no sound of stamping, restless horses in their stalls. No stable-boys cleaning up the yard – which it needed badly, Carrie thought. Even the gate was off its hinges.

As she stood staring at the neglected yard a man appeared round the corner of the stables. He walked with a shambling gait, weaving first right, then left. Drunkenness was no stranger to Carrie. She frequently saw its effects upon the navvies after every pay-out. And her pa, too.

As the man neared her, Carrie could see he was elderly with white wispy hair. His complexion was florid, almost purple, and his eyes bleary. He was grossly, uncomfortably overweight, and his ageing suit – once of fine material and well cut – now scarcely fitted him.

This must be Jamie's grandfather – Squire Trent.

He caught sight of her standing there watching him and he stopped and blinked, as if trying to focus his vision. Then he lurched towards her until he was standing in front of her. His gaze was fixed upon her face, then his mouth sagged open as he whispered brokenly. "Sarah!"

Carrie smiled uncertainly. "My name is Caroline – Carrie – Smithson."

"Caroline – Smithson? No – no, you're Sarah – my lovely Sarah!" He stretched out his arms and made as if to catch hold of her, but Carrie stepped back quickly.

"No – no, don't be afraid. I'll not . . ." he hiccupped and then belched noisily, "hurt you, Sarah. I'll not hurt you again."

"My name is not Sarah, it's . . ." Carrie stopped as the realisation struck her swiftly. Her grandmother's name was Sarah. Maybe her likeness to her grandmother was such that this old man, in his befuddled state, had turned back the years and mistaken her for Sarah Smithson.

But why, Carrie wondered, should Squire Trent address her grandmother in such a familiar, intimate manner?

Now he was rubbing his eyes with the back of his hand, miserably confused. "Caroline – not Sarah, not my Sarah? Then who are you. Why do you look like my love?"

His love? Carrie recoiled. Surely he could not be referring to her grandmother, that shrunken little old woman, careworn and with lines of bitterness engraved by the years upon her face?

At that moment there was the sound of a horse's hooves in the lane and Carrie saw Jamie cantering towards them. He slid from his mount and ran towards her, his dark eyes afire.

"Carrie – you've come, at last!"

Oblivious of his grandfather's presence he stood close to her, taking both her hands in his and raising them gently to his lips. The old man forgotten, Carrie gazed up into Jamie's eyes.

"I'm sorry," she said, excitement making her sound breathless. "I couldn't come – before. It was Luke – my brother. He was ill and I had to – look after him."

Jamie was smiling down at her. "I wondered why you did not come. But everything's all right now you're here."

"Yes," she whispered, their eyes still locked in a timeless gaze.

"Mus' be going," the old man muttered and shuffled away, his shoulders sagging with disappointment, but neither Carrie nor Jamie even glanced in his direction.

"Let me stable my horse and we'll go for a walk," Jamie said and Carrie nodded.

A little while later, their fingers interlaced, they were walking side by side up the lane towards the shady intimacy of the wood. Once beneath the sheltering trees, Jamie stopped and gently took her by the shoulders and turned her to face him. His lips brushed her forehead, her closed eyes and then found her mouth with a tender sweetness which thrilled her fast-beating heart. Never had she known such gentleness in a man. Certainly she had never seen it in her father, nor even in Lloyd Foster, who, despite his open admiration and desire for her, was brash in his approach.

Jamie's hands smoothed her long black hair and ran down her back coming to rest on her slender waist. Responding to his ardour, Carrie slipped her arms about his neck and pressed herself against his lithe, strong body. They could feel each other's heart beating through the thin clothes they wore this hot summer day.

Breathless they drew apart, their eyes afire with their new, overwhelming emotion.

"Oh, Carrie," he said softly, his fingers tracing the outline of her face. "My lovely, lovely Carrie," and he drew her once again into his embrace.

Much later they emerged from the wood, happiness shining from their faces.

"I must go back," Carrie murmured, but her words held no firm intention.

"No – stay. I can't bear to let you go now that I've found you. I didn't know one could fall in love so quickly." His eyes caressed her, making her heart sing. Never had she felt this way about any man before. So this was love and for Carrie, with her strong character, it was deep and lasting. "I didn't know it could be this way either," she whispered.

An hour later, Carrie, fearful her father's wrath would prevent further clandestine meetings with Jamie, said, "I really must go – but I'll try to come again tomorrow."

"I could come to your home . . ."

"No!" she said sharply, and then for fear her brusqueness had given offence, she put her hands upon his chest and stood on tiptoe to kiss him gently. "Not yet – I don't know what my folks would say. I don't want to tell them – yet."

Jamie smiled indulgently. "Yes, that's how I feel. I want it to be our own secret from all the world."

"Where – where shall I meet you?" she asked.

Jamie pointed. "How about the abbey ruins, mid-afternoon?"

Again he kissed her and then she was running up the hill out of Abbeyford.

Chpater Three

" 'Tis time we started on that little bit of a cutting to the north of the village and on the embankment through the valley itself, me boy."

They were standing at the edge of the woods, just above the Manor, overlooking Abbeyford village.

"Aye," Evan Smithson grinned. "Have you got the way-leave yet?"

Lloyd Foster rubbed his chin and laughed. "Yes – and no."

"What do you mean?"

"Yes, I've got the *way* planned, but not the 'leave'," and Evan joined in his laughter. "But I'm workin' on it, m'boy. The old man and me – we've got dis nice game o' cards goin'. Running up a peach of a debt to me, the man is." He shook his head. "Poor ol' divil, 'tis breakin' me heart, so it is!" But his grin belied his words.

Evan snorted. "Dunna waste your sympathy on *him*! He dunna deserve none."

Foster's eyes surveyed the line his railway would run. "And way over there," he mused, "to the south of the village, where there's that natural pass between the hills, we could have an unstaffed halt. Abbeyford Halt. I don't reckon it needs a station, for it'll only serve Abbeyford and Amberly."

Evan nodded with satisfaction. "Aye, an' it's still *his* land we'd be tekin'."

A girl was climbing the hill towards them, her head bent so as to avoid stubbing her bare feet on the rough ground.

"Isn't that me darlin' girl?" Foster narrowed his eyes against the bright sun.

Evan's mouth tightened. "Aye, it's Carrie. What the devil's she doin' here?"

Silently they watched her approach and it was not until she was almost up to them that she lifted her head and saw them.

She stopped and the joy disappeared from her face, her eyes darkened with fear and the smile faded from her lips as Evan stepped towards her menacingly. "Where've you been, girl?" Roughly he grasped hold of her arm.

Carrie winced but clenched her teeth against crying out. "To see me grandma," she lied glibly. Evan shook her. "Who gave you leave?"

"No – no one."

"You stay at home where you belong."

Carrie wrenched herself free and rubbed her arm. She turned to face him, her eyes blazing with anger now. "Home! You call that – that *hovel* – home?"

Evan's blow was swift and well aimed and before Carrie had time to spring back his hand had met her cheek like the crack of a pistol shot.

It was then that Lloyd Foster sprang forward, one arm went round Evan's throat in a vice-like grip, the other arm holding his arms behind his back. Evan gasped for breath as Foster, his mouth close to Evan's ear, all sign of joviality gone in a moment, muttered, "Don't you ever lay a finger on dat girl again, me boy. Not while I'm around. D'ya hear me now?"

Evan's face grew purple and he began to choke whilst Carrie watched in amazement at the sudden change in Lloyd Foster's manner.

"D'you *hear*?" he asked again, jerking his arm even tighter around Evan's throat. Evan's 'yes' was little more than a squeak.

"Dat's better," Foster released his hold and turned to Carrie, his face still unsmiling. "You'd best be off home, me lovely. I'll talk to yer da."

Carrie glanced once at her father – once was enough to read the malice in his eyes.

She turned and ran.

For a few moments Foster watched her until she disappeared amongst the trees, then he turned back to Evan. He laid his hand on his shoulder, now in a gesture of friendship. "Ach, I'm sorry about that, me boy. But – I have dis feeling for dat girl of yours, don't you know?"

"She's still *my* daughter," Evan said gruffly, more angry to have been made to look foolish in front of Carrie than over the physical hurt Foster had momentarily inflicted.

"I know, I know," Foster's tone was placating now, his hand still on Evan's shoulder. "But I have this plan in me mind. Maybe I'd better be telling you about it." He paused and then went on. "Ye see, I want that girl of yours. I've a mind to wed her."

He let his words sink into Evan's mind before he went on again. "And I want to strike out for pastures new. England's too small. There's a whole *world* out there waiting – just waiting for me railroads. You see, me darlin' boy, what I t'ought was dis. If you'll give me the hand of yer lovely daughter in holy matrimony, we'll be away across the seas to make our fortunes. And," he stood back facing Evan as he delivered the final coup, "And I'll be givin' *you* the contract I hold to build the rest of *this* railway! Now, what d'you say to that, me boy?"

Evan stared at him for several moments in total disbelief. "You'll *give* me the contract?"

"Aye."

"Why in hell's name should you give me anything?"

Foster spread his hands wide and cast his eyes heavenwards in a gesture of mock despair. "An' haven't I been tellin' you, you'll be givin' me your daughter. An' to my way of t'inking, I'll be getting the best o' the bargain. Oh," he rolled his eyes, "to see dat lovely girl dressed in silks and satins. She'll be like a queen, she will, to be sure."

Evan's eyes glittered suddenly and he turned his gaze away from Foster to look down at the village of Abbeyford.

"Then," he murmured more to himself than to Foster, "it'll be *me* building the railway across his land!"

There was silence. Then Evan turned and held out his hand to Lloyd Foster. "It's a bargain!"

Foster clasped Evan's hand delightedly and his ready laugh rang out across the hills.

Carrie waited in fear for the return of her father that evening, trying to think of a way to avoid him. The shack was so cramped that unless she were to go somewhere right away there was no escape.

But Evan appeared in a very jovial, hearty mood, surprising not only Carrie but her mother and brothers too. Far from berating her further, he kept glancing at his daughter and grinning as if sharing some secret with her. Carrie and her mother exchanged looks and Carrie lifted her shoulders in a shrug, signifying that she, too, was mystified by her father's unusually good mood.

Since her father had not questioned her any more about her visits to Abbeyford, Carrie's desire and love for Jamie, which daily grew stronger, made her risk another visit the following afternoon.

She followed the lane up towards the Manor and as she rounded a bend she saw ahead of her the gig belonging to Lady Lynwood. Seated in the stationary gig was Lady Adelina and her daughter, Francesca, and beside the vehicle nearest the girl was Jamie Trent on horseback. He was smiling down at Francesca, who, with her head thrown back and laughter on her lips, was the picture of elegant loveliness.

Carrie felt an almost physical pain in her breast. Jealousy swept through her in an overwhelming wave, making her feel quite dizzy. Quietly she crept through a gap in the hedge and moved silently along until she was level with the gig, though hidden by the hedge. Now she could hear their conversation.

"We have not seen you of late, Jamie," Francesca was saying in a purring tone. "You have neglected us shamefully, has he not, Mama?"

Peering through the leafy hedge, Carrie saw Lady Lynwood smile gently. "I guess you've been real busy on the farm, Jamie?"

Jamie nodded and there was a trace of grimness in his tone.

"I'm afraid so. We're losing workers to the towns, to say nothing of the land we've lost."

"Oh, Jamie, I'm so sorry. Is there anything we can do to help?"

Jamie shrugged and sighed. "No. I don't reach the age of twenty-five – when I can take over completely – for another two years. If only no more goes before then, we may pull through."

Carrie closed her eyes and almost groaned aloud. Lloyd Foster and her father planned to take more land from Jamie, she knew. But these thoughts were driven from her mind again as she saw him lean down towards the gig and take Francesca's hand in his.

"I must go, my dear. I'll try to visit soon –I promise." He raised her gloved hand to his lips.

"Now don't go breaking that promise, Mr Trent, or I shall be mightily put out!" The girl teased, laughing up at him flirtatiously.

Carrie knew nothing of the ways of Society, of coquetry or gentle, meaningless, flirting, so her heart twisted with pain and jealousy. There was something between that girl and her Jamie! Jamie rode off in one direction and Lady Adelina slapped the reins, and the gig moved off in the other. Carrie saw Francesca turn round to wave again to Jamie and saw his return wave and she closed her eyes to shut out the picture.

She sat down where she was, behind the hedge at the edge of a meadow and tore angrily at the long grass with her fingers. How dare he? How can he make love to me one moment and then be so affectionate towards that girl? Hate began to grow in Carrie's heart for the girl she hardly knew. A few moments later she sprang to her feet and ran and ran until her lungs were bursting, up the lane, through the wood to the abbey ruins. Only then did she sink down against the crumbling walls, panting and sobbing.

Impatient with herself for shedding tears, Carrie rubbed at her eyes with the back of her hand. Gradually her misery turned to anger against Jamie. She waited and waited. An hour went by and still he did not come. When at last she saw his horse appear out of the trees and canter towards her, even the sight of him, which caused her heart to beat a little faster in spite of her anger, could not wipe away the picture of him with Francesca.

"Where've you been? You're late," she greeted him crossly. "I've been waiting an hour or more."

"I'm sorry, my darling." He came to her and tried to take her in his arms but she pushed him away.

"I'm not your slave, your plaything to be picked up and put down just when you feel like it!"

"Carrie, Carrie . . ."

"I saw you with – with – *her*!"

Jamie frowned. "What are you talking about?"

"With Francesca. Mighty friendly you seemed to be!" Carrie stood, her hands on her hips, her feet planted wide apart, her violet eyes flashing now, her wild hair flying, quite unconscious of how lovely she looked – a natural, untamed beauty.

Jamie gazed at her admiringly. "My dear," he said softly. "Lady Lynwood was once my stepmother, and Francesca and I are like brother and sister."

"Huh! It didn't look like that to me!" Carrie retorted. "Fluttering her long eyelashes at you, making up to you. You forgot all about meeting me here, didn't you? Didn't you?"

"Carrie, my dear love. I've come at the same time as always. It's only three o'clock. You must have been early."

Then she remembered. She had been so distressed by the scene in the lane that she had completely forgotten to pay her usual visit to her grandmother's cottage before coming to the abbey ruins to meet Jamie.

Suddenly her anger evaporated and she flung herself against him, throwing her arms about him. "Oh Jamie, I'm sorry. Forgive me."

"My darling girl. There, there," he said, stroking her hair and, gently tilting her head back, he kissed her ardently.

Carrie felt him lift her into his arms and carry her the short distance towards the one small cell-like room left whole in the abbey ruins. They squeezed through the small opening. Inside it was dim and quiet.

They kissed with growing passion, lost in their own secret world, their embrace all the sweeter after the misunderstanding between them. His fingers gently unfastened the buttons of her coarse blouse and caressed her. Swept away on a tide of love they gave themselves to one another in mutual desire. Jamie's lovemaking was so gentle and thoughtful that – virgin though she was – Carrie felt no pain, only an overwhelming need to give herself to this wonderfully considerate man.

Afterwards they lay in each other's arms, the tempest of their ardour subsiding to a calm feeling of closeness.

"I know so little about you," Jamie murmured, his lips warm against her neck, "and yet I know that I love you, my dearest Carrie."

She ran her fingers through his brown hair. "You're the first man I've loved," she told him, almost shyly.

"I know," he whispered, "and I'm glad – so glad."

"My first love and my last love."

"Oh, Carrie, Carrie," and his mouth found hers again. "We must be together always. Marry me, my darling. Be my wife."

"Yes – oh, yes," she breathed and closed her eyes. There could be no greater happiness on earth, she thought, than this moment.

The weeks of that hot, ardent summer faded into autumn. Lloyd Foster made ready to begin work on the cutting needed about a mile north of Abbeyford and the embankment through the valley itself.

"We take on more men, Evan me boy," he explained. "See the village men. If what I hear is true, they'll be only too glad of the work. Seems the Trents only employ a few now and the next estate – Lord Lynwood's, is it?"

Evan nodded.

"Well, he employs men from his own village – Amberly. Is that right?"

"Yes, but I'd have thought he'd have employed Abbeyford men on the land Lord Royston left his daughter Francesca."

"Is that the pretty girl with an older but still lovely lady I see riding about in a foine carriage?"

"Aye. Lady Lynwood and her daughter. They were lookin' for you some time back."

"Were dey now? Now isn't that the greatest shame I missed meeting them? But, then, they can't hold a candle to me darlin' Carrie's lovely face. Ah – if she had dose fine clothes an' a carriage, wouldn't she be the grand lady too, I'm t'inkin'?"

"Takes more'n clothes and carriages to make a lady of someone," Evan growled, bitterness clouding his eyes. "Takes birth and breeding."

Foster laughed. "An' what would me navvy ganger be worryin' about that for, eh?"

"There's things you dunna know, Foster, even yet!" Abruptly, Evan Smithson changed the subject. "I'll see the village men – but then what?"

"We divide the men into three gangs. One lot to continue working on the flat bed where we are now, one lot to begin work on the embankment and the third gang to work a cutting through that little incline between the two. That'll not take as long to do as the embankment in the valley and by the time that's finished the line should be nearly ready to join up."

Evan thought rapidly. He could not fault the scheme but he knew he would be hard pressed to keep tight control over three gangs of navvies working some three miles apart. As if reading his thoughts, Foster said, "Start training two or three to take over as gangers soon. I plan to see this little scheme started and see you have no problems but I'll be away with me lovely bride before it's done."

Evan found that Foster had spoken the truth about the Abbeyford men. Many were unemployed now and bitterness against the Trents – Squire Trent especially, since it was his gambling debts which had caused their possessions to dwindle – was growing.

"Aw, Evan lad," Joby Robinson, son of the village smithy whom he'd known in boyhood, greeted him. "The years 'ave proved you right. We should have won our battle all them years ago, not given in just because Wallis Trent called out the yeomanry. Lad, if we'd tried again after he was killed, we'd 'ave won! But you'd gone – disappeared."

"Aye, I thought it best. I thought I'd not be welcome after the bloodshed that night."

"Aye, well, 'appen. Straight after, we was all bitter – that's true. But we're worse off now than ever."

Evan grinned. "Well – I've work for as many as wants it."

"Aw, lad, that's great."

"It's hard graft, mind," Evan warned, "and since I'm boss, I'll not stand for shirkers."

"They'll come, we'll all come, lad, and thank you for it."

So the Abbeyford men – the unemployed, that is – from at first resenting the encroaching railway, now seized upon its arrival as a gift from God. Hungry mouths could be fed once more and a man could have back his pride he had felt to be lost. Yet those who still worked on the Trents' land saw the railway as a further threat to their already insecure livelihood and began to look upon those village men who had become gangers as turncoats.

Abbeyford became a divided village.

There were just two matters left to settle before the new workings could actually begin – the acquisition of part of the Trents' lands, indeed the majority of the land still left in their possession, and Foster's acquisition of Carrie Smithson in exchange for giving Evan Smithson the rest of the contract.

The first came about quite easily, for Foster had prepared well in advance for that very event, though the aftermath was to cause such a turbulence that the ripples would be felt for years to come.

Foster had joined a card school where Squire Trent frequently played. By making himself a good friend to the drink-sodden, sad old man, Lloyd Foster had by now manoeuvred him into a helpless position. To repay his gambling debts to Foster, Squire Trent was obliged to sell off yet more of his land. And with Foster's blarney he made it seem as if he were doing the old man a favour instead of a disastrous disservice.

"Didn't I tell you I could do it?" Lloyd Foster boasted, waving a piece of paper under Evan's nose. "An' all legal-like too!"

"How much have you got?" Evan's eyes gleamed as he grabbed the paper out of Foster's fingers and scanned it eagerly.

"My God!" he exclaimed when he saw the figures written there. "Twice as much acreage as I thought you'd get and at half the price I thought you'd have to pay!" He looked up at Foster admiringly. "You crafty devil!" he grinned.

Foster laughed and slapped Evan on the back. "An' it's all in your hands now, me boy. 'Course the land belongs to the Railway Board, they laid out the money, you know that, don't you?"

Evan nodded. "Of course."

"And now," Foster said softly, "the contract's yours."

"The Board agreed, then?"

"They did too. When I saw them in Manchester last week about that," he jabbed his forefinger at the paper Evan still held, "I told them I was wantin' to spread me wings and fly like an eagle."

"And they let you go – without working out your contract?" Evan showed surprise.

"Didn't I tell them you were me right-hand man, that you knew as much about the building of dis railroad as me, and that, as long as the engineer checks everything, they'll have their railroad on schedule, if not before? By the way, they want to see you next week – just to make it all official."

Evan nodded. He'd had little cause in his life to thank any man for favours, and now he found his gratitude to this man impossible to express. But the irrepressible Irishman needed no thanks. "An' you'll not be forgetting your side of the bargain, now, will you, me boy?" For a moment, beneath the banter, there was the hint of steel.

"No – no," Evan said swiftly, trying to sound reassuring, but even he could not be sure his wayward daughter would comply.

During the first weeks of autumn Carrie and Jamie, locked in the bliss of their growing love, each living only for the next moment when they would meet and touch and hold each other close, had been oblivious of the world around them. For Carrie it was an escape from the harsh reality she knew into a dream of tenderness and joy she had never believed could exist. Even Jamie, entranced by Carrie – this wild beauty like no other girl he had ever known – forgot, for a time, his drunken grandfather, his sullen employees, the dwindling estate, and the threatening railway over the hill.

Now, cruel reality was crowding in upon their private world.

It was pay-out night and the navvies descended into Abbeyford like a band of marauding Red Indians. They wanted liquor and because Lloyd Foster was an employer who believed that he could extract better work from his men by giving them what they wanted from time to time he had arranged that a quantity of ale was on hand.

So it was a drunken, rowdy mob who ran, whooping and yelling, down the hillside into the peaceful village below, looking for sport of any kind. They were rough, tough men who worked hard and played hard too.

"Come on out, you village wenches," shouted one banging on the door of a cottage, whilst behind the door a mother clasped her young daughters to her, her eyes wide with fear. "Hush," she whispered fearful that the girls' terrified whimperings would be heard. "Be quiet and he'll go away."

After a few moments, unable to gain any response, the navvy staggered round to the rear of the cottage, where he found half a dozen hens in a run.

"Aha, lookee what we have here. You'll mek me a foine dinner, I'm thinkin'," and he began to chase the birds, which, feathers flying, ran hither and thither, squawking loudly.

"Come here, blast you, you silly critters," he muttered rolling from side to side, making feeble grasping movements.

"What is it you're doin', Joseph me boy?"

Three more navvies, hearing the commotion, had gravitated towards the noise and now stood, a little unsteadily, watching their friend.

"Tryin' to catch dees stupid birds, so I am!"

"Well, let us be helpin' you." And the three of them climbed into the chicken run. Drunk though the men were, the chickens were no match for four pairs of grasping hands and very soon all six birds lay in a twitching heap, their necks broken.

"Now – der's one each for us and two over – is dat right? We can sell them other two, I'm t'inkin'."

"Aye an' do you know what I'm t'inkin', Joseph?"

"No, Michael, and what might dat be?"

"If dis 'ere cottage has chickens, maybe der's others in the village too, eh? What d'you t'ink?"

Joseph blinked, swaying on his feet.

"I t'ink you could be right. Come on."

Between the four of them they killed fifty-four chickens that night and carried them off in sacks up the hill back to the dwelling-place.

Another small group of navvies smashed the windows of the Monks Arms because the landlord refused to serve them any more ale. So they hurled stones at his windows and then burst into the bar and helped themselves. With even more drink inside them they rampaged down the one village street, tearing up plants from the gardens, damaging fences and gates and hurling stones through windows. Not until dawn began to stretch its pale fingers over the skyline did the navvies stagger back up the hill.

The following afternoon Carrie waited in the abbey ruins for Jamie. She shivered and drew her tattered shawl more closely about her. It was a blustery, cool day with grey clouds scudding overhead.

She saw him approach and ran to meet him as he tethered his horse and dismounted.

"Oh, Jamie – is it only yesterday since I saw you? It seems so long ago." She flung herself against him and as he put his arms about her she could feel a fierceness in his embrace. She raised her head to look up at him. His eyes were dark with anger and his mouth was set in a hard line.

"Jamie, what is it? Something's wrong, I know it."

Jamie tried to smile. " 'Tis naught to do with you, sweetheart. It's those – those railway workers."

Carrie stiffened and her heart missed a beat. Sure though she was now of Jamie's love for her, still she had not been able to

44

bring herself to tell him of her own connection with the railway. She had not dared to risk spoiling their idyllic happiness.

"What – what has happened?"

"They descended on Abbeyford village last night, an unruly *mob*!" He clenched his teeth. "They've caused damage to property and stolen hens and frightened the women and girls half out of their wits."

"Was – was anyone hurt?"

He hesitated then said, "One girl was raped."

Carrie groaned.

"The village men – those who are not involved with the railway themselves – are out for revenge. I can see trouble brewing. I'd like to get my hands on the men responsible for those – those drunken louts!"

Carrie shuddered and wound her arms tightly about Jamie, burying her face against his chest. She felt him relax a little. She raised her head and looked up at him. He cupped her face in his hands and looked deep into her violet eyes. "Oh, my darling – what should I do without you now? You are the only one who brings me happiness."

His mouth was upon hers, their bodies entwined and for the moment all other thoughts were driven from their minds save the sweet passion flaring between them.

When they parted some two hours later, Jamie to return to the Manor and Carrie to run, skipping and jumping with light-hearted happiness, she had almost forgotten his mood of anger and even Jamie was smiling once more as he waved farewell.

"I won't, I won't – *I won't*!" Carrie shouted and stamped her foot.

Only moments before she had been dancing over the fields from her tryst with Jamie, giddy with happiness and her love for him. And now she stood in the centre of the rough shack facing her father, her violet eyes flashing with rage, her hands clenched so that the nails dug into her palms.

"You'll do as you're told, my girl," Evan spat, grasping her long black hair and wrenching her head back, whilst he raised his other hand to deal her a stinging blow.

"Whatever you do to me," Carrie said through her teeth, "you can't *make* me marry Lloyd Foster."

"You'll obey your pa, my girl," Evan bellowed again giving her hair a vicious tug, "or . . ."

"Never – never," Carrie screamed and twisting sideways, she sank her white teeth into his arm. His hold on her slackened. "You little she-cat! Why, I'll kill you . . ."

But Carrie did not wait to hear any more threats. She flung herself against the door of the shack, wrenching it open with such force that the rotten woodwork trembled and splintered. But as she hurled herself through the doorway, she came up against something solid – something, or rather someone, tall and broad and strong, whose arms were about her lifting her off her feet and swinging her round.

"Ah, an' if it isn't me darling running to meet me with a welcome I didn't expect."

Then, as Carrie realised it was Lloyd Foster holding her fast, she began to beat down upon his shoulders and kick at his legs.

"Now, now, this was not the welcome I had in mind." Still holding her, he glanced towards Evan, who had appeared in the doorway of the shack, holding his arm.

Then behind Foster there came the sound of horse's hooves and all at once Carrie's flailing arms and kicking legs were stilled and Foster felt her body go rigid in his arms. He looked into her face and saw her violet eyes widen with fear. Huskily she whispered a name.

"Jamie! *Oh, no!*"

Lloyd Foster lowered her slowly to the ground and turned to follow the line of her horrified gaze. He saw a young man, tall and broad-shouldered, his skin tanned, his handsome face contorted with anger, leaping down from his horse.

Then Foster saw, as the young man caught sight of Carrie, the rage soften momentarily in his eyes, heard him speak her name in surprise.

"Carrie? What on earth ...?" An expression of bewilderment flickered over the young fellow's face as he glanced away from her, towards Evan Smithson still standing in the doorway of the rough shack, briefly took in Lloyd Foster and then returned to Carrie's face.

Carrie, breaking free of the paralysing shock, ran towards the young man, the tears running down her face.

Never, Lloyd Foster thought dully, in all the time he had known her – through all the misery of her hard life and her father's brutality – never had he seen her weep. And now the girl whom, in his own boisterous way, he loved, was running towards another man, her arms outstretched, crying out to him with an impassioned plea. "Jamie, Jamie – you must take me away with you. You must save me. He's trying to make me marry Lloyd Foster. Tell him ..." She flung herself against him and clung to him, but Jamie Trent, like a man in a daze, merely stared over her head at Evan Smithson and Lloyd Foster. "Tell him I belong to you."

Jamie's eyes were hard, his mouth a grim line as he took hold of her arms and released himself from her limpet hold upon him. He held her away from him by the shoulders. He looked into her tearstained face, not an ounce of sympathy in his expression.

"You belong here? To the railway people?" His voice was harsh.

The hope died on Carrie's face. She closed her eyes and groaned aloud. "I can't help that. Jamie – I love you."

He thrust her aside and walked towards where Lloyd Foster and Evan Smithson stood watching. Behind him – unobserved by any of them now – Carrie sank to the ground and buried her face in her hands.

"Who's the contractor?" Jamie Trent demanded.

Foster and Evan exchanged a glance.

"Well, 'tis like this, d'you see. I am – but I'm in the process of handing the remainder of the contract over to Mr Smithson here. So – perhaps if you were to tell the both of us what it is troubling you, me boy."

"Are you Foster?"

"I am dat. Me fame must be spreadin' far an' wide," he grinned.

47

"Fame?" Jamie's lip curled. "Is that what you call it? Infamy more like!"

Foster, instead of being insulted, threw back his head and roared with laughter. For a moment Jamie seemed disconcerted and then his anger grew as he thought his grievance was not being taken seriously.

"You've swindled an old man – a drunken, confused old man – out of his – and my – inheritance. There's not enough land left now to be worth the working!"

Evan Smithson's eyes glittered and a slow smile spread across his mouth. He folded his arms and leant against the door-frame.

"Drunk as ever, then, is he?" he said quietly.

Jamie met his gaze squarely and for a moment there was silence as the two men stared at each other: one, young, angry and a little unsure of himself; the other, older by some twenty or more years, a self-satisfied expression on his face.

"You – you know my grandfather?"

Evan Smithson continued to stare disconcertingly into the young man's troubled eyes.

Quietly and deliberately, Evan said, "I should do. I'm his son!"

Chapter Four

The reactions to Evan's dramatic statement were varied.

"Well now," Foster murmured softly. "An' don't that be explaining a lot o' t'ings."

Jamie Trent was motionless, his stare fixed upon Evan. His tanned face turned pale.

Carrie raised her head slowly, disbelievingly, from her hands, her sobs stilled in shock. Her violet eyes, still brimming with tears, gazed at her father and then at Jamie's rigid back. "Oh, no," she whispered hoarsely. "No, no, *no!*" her voice rising to hysteria.

"His – *son?*" Jamie Trent's voice was no more than a whisper. "But how – who . . .?"

The enormity of Evan's words seemed to dawn upon the bewildered young man. "You mean – you're illegitimate!" he said baldly.

Evan's mouth tightened and his eyes hardened. "Aye, Squire Trent's bastard by a village girl."

Slowly Jamie nodded as understanding came. "Sarah Smithson." And the way in which he uttered her name told the onlookers that the revelation of these facts answered questions which had puzzled him for years.

There was no need for confirmation – they all realised the truth of Jamie's statement.

Not that gentle little old woman in the cottage and that drunken old man – it wasn't possible! Carrie closed her eyes and rocked to and fro on her haunches. And yet they, too, must have been young once, must have laughed and loved in secret – just as she and Jamie had done.

"So," Jamie was saying, "you'd bring ruin to your own father, would you?"

Evan stepped close to him, his eyes filled with hatred, only inches from Jamie's, so close that Jamie could feel the spittle rain upon his face as Evan spat out the words. "Father? *Father?* What sort of father has he been to me? Look at the ruin he's brought to people's lives. Ruined a pretty young village girl. Ruined Henry Smithson's life – to say nothing of mine. I've waited years for this moment – all me life! So don't expect no sympathy from me. I'll see the whole lot o' you in hell first!"

He turned his back on Jamie and strode away towards the railway, as if he would push the line – single – handed – through the Trents' land, so deep was his bitter desire for revenge.

For a moment Jamie seemed too stunned to move, then suddenly he turned and ran to his horse and mounted. Ignoring Carrie's desperate cry, "Jamie, oh Jamie!" he rode away at a breakneck gallop.

Carrie watched him go through a blur of tears, the sobs shaking her body. She felt a hand upon her shoulder.

"Don't, me darlin', don't," Lloyd Foster said, gently comforting. He drew her, unresisting, to her feet and put his arms about her. Hardly realising who was offering her support, Carrie clung to him, still weeping brokenly. He stroked her hair and rocked her. Then suddenly she tore herself free and rushed into the shack. Lloyd Foster watched her go with misery in his eyes. Slowly he turned away and followed Evan's path to the railway. The railway! There was still the railway . . .

That evening, before Evan returned home, Carrie slipped away from the shack. Lucy, unable to help her daughter, for after years of misery and hardship she had no strength to fight any more, watched her go with unhappy eyes. Calm now, Carrie was resolved to seek out Jamie.

"It doesn't matter that we're cousins," she said aloud to herself as she tramped determinedly across the hills towards Abbeyford.

"In Society circles lots of cousins marry. It doesn't *matter!*" She tried to convince herself.

There was a cold October wind blowing and, by the time she neared the Manor House, Carrie was shivering. She drew the old shawl closer round her shoulders and slipped through the stableyard gate. There was no movement in the yard, no light from the windows on this side of the house. She moved towards the back door which she guessed led into the kitchens. Her heart was pounding now. She was afraid she would meet with some servant who would bar the way of the gypsy girl, but no one came to impede her entry to the house. She pushed open the door and went in. She stopped a moment, waiting whilst her eyes accustomed themselves to the dimness. She felt her way through the kitchen and up the stairs leading to the upper house. Through the swing door cutting off the servants' domain from the main part of the house, and into the entrance hall. Here a candelabrum burnt, casting eerie shadows. A grandfather clock ticked heavily in the corner, but the whole place was as neglected inside as outside in the stable-yard. Dust covered the furniture and the floor was dull and mud-stained. Carrie jumped as she heard a shuffling noise and turned to see an old man moving towards her, his back so bent he could hardly lift his head to look at her.

"What do you want?" He was dressed in a shabby black suit and Carrie guessed he must be a servant of sorts, probably the only one who remained in the service of the Trents now.

"I want to see Mr Jamie Trent, please," Carrie said boldly, drawing herself up and trying to sound as if she had every right to be there.

"He's gone," the old man sniffed.

"G-gone? Where's he gone?"

"How should I know? Went galloping off on his horse as if the devil himself were after him."

"Is – is Squire Trent here?" Her tone was more hesitant now.

"Oh, yes." The man stretched his mouth into the semblance of a grin. "Drinking himself into his usual stupor." He waved his hand towards the left-hand side of the hall and said, his tone heavy with sarcasm, "The Master is in his study, ma'am, if you'd care to step this way!"

Opening the door he indicated and peering round it, she saw Squire Guy Trent slumped over his desk, an empty glass in one hand and an empty bottle at his elbow. This room, too, was dusty and littered with papers, empty bottles and dirty glasses.

Carrie cleared her throat, but when there was no response from him she moved closer.

"Squire Trent?" Still no reply, so tentatively she put her hand on his shoulder.

"Wha' . . .?" His movement was so sudden that Carrie snatched her hand away in fright and sprang back a pace.

Bleary eyes gazed up at her, his head rolling from side to side. "Who is it? Can't see . . ."

"It's Carrie. Carrie Smithson." She bent closer now, desperation giving her courage. After all, he was only drunk and hadn't she seen *that* many times before?

"Squire – where's Jamie?"

"Carrie? Carrie Smithson?"

"Yes. Where's Jamie? I must see Jamie. It's – important!"

"Jamie?" he repeated stupidly, whilst Carrie grew more impatient.

"Yes. Where is he?"

"I don't know. Gone. Gone away. Left me."

"What do you mean?"

"Left me all alone. He was in a rage. Wouldn't speak to me. Looked as if he – he could – kill me. Never been frightened of Jamie before. Not Jamie. Wallis, yes. I was always afraid of Wallis. My own son – and I was afraid of him." The words were drawling and slurred but Carrie could plainly understand. She sat down in a chair opposite the desk. She would have to be patient with him if she were to learn anything. Perhaps if she encouraged him to ramble on like this, she would find out what she wanted to know.

"Your son, Jamie's father?" she prompted.

"Yes. He was a hard man, so cold and ruthless! I've been a failure all my life. Failed my parents, failed my wife and son and worst of all, I failed the only girl I ever really loved. My Sarah!"

Carrie said gently. "Jamie knows about – about you and Sarah. My father told him."

"Your father?" The eyes peered at her, red and puffy.

"Yes. Evan Smithson. Your – son by Sarah."

For a moment the room was still and silent. Then the old man let out such a groan that Carrie was afraid. He covered his face with his hands, knocking over the bottle, which rolled to the edge of the desk and fell to the floor, shattering into a dozen pieces. The glass dropped from his fingers to the desk, but Carrie grabbed it before it, too, fell to the floor. He was panting and moaning and Carrie thought the shock had brought on a heart attack of some kind.

"I'm sorry," she said swiftly. "I'm terribly sorry. But please – you must help me. I love Jamie. And he loves me, I know he does," she tried to convince herself, blotting out the picture of him riding away from her, ignoring her when he had learnt the dreadful truth.

The pathetic old man seemed suddenly, painfully sober. Slowly his hands fell away from his face, his moaning quietened and he looked at Carrie full in the face. "As I loved Sarah and she loved me."

There was silence. Moved by pity, Carrie reached out her hand and touched the old man's. He covered hers with his other hand. "If you love him, and he loves you, let no one stand in the way of your happiness. No one! Do you hear me?"

Carrie nodded, unable to speak for the lump in her throat. "But," she whispered at last, "he rode off without a word – after – after Pa had told him. Perhaps . . ."

"It'll be all right. He was hurt. Hurt beyond words, but he'll get over it." Squire Trent, for a brief moment, was no longer the pathetic drunk, but an elderly gentleman offering comfort to a distressed young girl – his granddaughter. That fact seemed suddenly to dawn upon him. "You're – you're my granddaughter, then?"

"I – suppose so," Carrie said and smiled faintly at him. His grasp upon her hand tightened.

"Don't let anyone or anything stand in the way of your love," he said hoarsely, "or you'll spend your life lost and alone – like I have done. I fell in love with Sarah, but I was the squire's son! My parents arranged for me to marry Louisa Marchant, the daughter of a wealthy clothing manufacturer from Manchester. I tried to fight them, tried to see Sarah. But they were all against us. Her father – Joseph Miller – arranged for her to marry a distant cousin – Henry Smithson. But I still might have won," he thumped the table with his fist, "but I was attacked in the wood late one night." He glanced at Carrie sheepishly. "I was drunk. Seems as if I've been drunk ever since," he muttered and then his voice grew stronger again. "I never saw who attacked me, but while I lay abed – my Sarah married Smithson and – and my father sent Joseph Miller to gaol!"

Carrie gasped. "Sarah's father? Why?"

Squire Trent groaned and closed his eyes. "He *said* it was because he believed it was Miller who attacked me."

"And was it?"

He shrugged. "We've never found out. He wouldn't admit it – nor would he defend himself. But he was a strong man, a man who stood up against my father for his rights, and my father hated him. Of course, he died in gaol, and Sarah's mother died soon after. Broke the whole family. They've hated me ever since. Your father – my own son – he's had the hate bred into him. He led the village against the Manor once. Wallis was killed."

"I know," Carrie said. "I heard about that."

"And now he's ruined me – and Jamie – completely."

There was silence again.

Carrie said gently, "Where do you think Jamie went?"

Sadly, he shook his head. "I don't know. I thought maybe he'd gone for good, but perhaps if there's you to come back for ..." He left the sentence hanging in the air like an unanswered question.

His head fell forward again. "I'm tired," he said heavily. "So tired of it all."

Carrie left him sleeping over the desk.

That night Carrie hid in the Manor stables, waiting in case Jamie should return. But at the first light of dawn, when she awoke from a fitful doze to move her cramped, cold limbs there was still no horse back in the stall, no sign of Jamie.

She couldn't – wouldn't – go home. But where could she go? Not her grandmother's – her father would think to look for her there. The abbey ruins! Jamie would come to her there. It was their meeting-place. The place where they had made love and spent their moments of bliss. Her cold, cramped feet moved faster and faster and she began to run both to warm herself and to reach the abbey ruins all the quicker. Why had she not thought of it before? she scolded herself. Jamie would come for her there – she was certain of it!

"Where is she?" Lloyd Foster demanded.

"How should I know?" Evan replied.

Foster's face showed none of its usual geniality. He grasped Evan's shirt collar and hauled him close. Though sturdy and strong, Evan was no match for the big Irishman. "Then you'd better be findin' her, me boy. A bargain's a bargain. I've no mind to lose that little girl, d'you hear me now?"

"She'll come back," Evan said confidently.

"How can you be so sure?"

"Because he's gone."

"Young Trent?"

"Aye."

"How can you be sure she hasn't gone with him?"

"Yesterday – after he rode off in such a tekin' – she was at home all day until just before I got home. Me wife said so."

"So? She could still have gone to find him."

Patiently, Evan said, "No, it was me went after Jamie Trent. In the afternoon he was at the workings talking to Luke, but I soon put a stop to that. I told him she was to marry you. That it'd be no good cousins marrying – enough bad blood on both sides to breed the devil himself!"

"What did he say?"

Evan laughed. "He looked sick – sick and beaten!"

"But what was he saying to Luke, maybe he was arranging to meet her – through Luke, eh?"

"Nay. I asked Luke an' he said he'd only just come as I got there. Trent hadn't said nothing."

"He could be lying. Lyin' to protect Carrie."

Evan frowned. "Luke – lie to me? He wouldn't dare!"

Foster gave a grunt of disbelief. "Frightened of you he may be, me boy, but he thinks a lot of his sister. Maybe more than his fear of you."

Foster said no more but strode away leaving Evan frowning thoughtfully.

"Luke, come here."

Luke Smithson glanced fearfully at his father. They were at the new workings of the Abbeyford embankment. He had put Luke in charge of the gangers on this section, but the sick, weak boy had no power to be authoritative over the men.

Luke slid down the bank and came towards Evan.

"You sure young Trent said naught to you?"

Two spots of colour appeared in the boy's cheeks and he coughed. "Nay," he gasped, "I told you, didn't I? You came up just as he got off his horse. He'd no time to say aught . . ."

"You'd better not be lyin' to me, boy, or it'll be the worse for you. Now get back and shape these men up. You'll let 'em run riot over you, if you dunna."

Thankfully Luke turned his back on his father and hurried away, feeling, as he did so, the rustle of paper in his pocket. The letter Jamie Trent had given him for Carrie. How long he could keep it from his pa, he didn't know. He just wished Carrie would come home so he could give it to her and be done with it!

Then all thoughts of Carrie and Jamie Trent and even of his father's wrath were swept from his mind as his gaze travelled up the hill above the embankment.

Ranged in a line some hundred yards away, silent, watchful and menacing stood thirty or more men armed with a variety of weapons – picks, shovels, staffs, crooks and knives. The navvies had seen them and had paused in their work, looking up at the strangers above them.

The farmworkers, Luke thought, and shuddered. They've come to try to stop us building the railway through their village. For a moment he closed his eyes and when he opened them the men had begun to move slowly forward down the incline towards the railway workings. The navvies, too, had, by common, silent consent formed themselves into a defensive line and they stood waiting, watching the approach of their adversaries. It was like two armies in a battle, Luke thought, and then the two lines met and clashed. Screams and cries and the sound of wood on wood and metal against metal filled the air and there was no more time for conscious thought!

Lloyd Foster sat on his horse at the top of the hill overlooking the quiet, peaceful village of Abbeyford.

"Where could she have gone, where could she be hidin' herself?" he murmured aloud, his gaze roaming the countryside, taking in the squat, straggly cottages, the grand mansion, Abbeyford Grange and the neglected Manor House, and the mounds of earth already beginning to form the embankment which would run right across the valley. Then his eyes came to rest on the abbey ruins to his right, rising gaunt and black against the grey October sky. He spurred his horse and galloped across the ridge towards the ruins, feeling the first spots of rain on his face from the low, threatening clouds above.

Carrie crouched down in the small, cell-like room in the ruins. She had been there since early morning. She was cold and hungry and so miserable. If only Jamie would come! She had ventured out once or twice to peer over the crumbling walls, hoping for sight of him. But the fields were empty, devoid even of workers. She dare not show herself in the open for fear someone might see her. So the little room, cold and inhospitable it seemed now – so different from the sanctuary it had been when she had lain in Jamie's arms – had become her hideout.

During the late afternoon the room became darker as rain clouds gathered. Carrie crouched against the wall, dozing fitfully, worn out with the drama of the past few hours.

As if in a dream she heard the horse's hoofbeats.

"Jamie, Jamie! He's come!" She dragged herself, still dazed, but hopeful now, to the doorway. The rain beat upon her face, arousing her to full wakefulness as she saw a man climbing over the low wall. She watched him jump down into the ruins and come towards her.

She stretched out her hands and made to run towards him. "Jamie! Oh, Jamie!"

"Oh, an' there you are, me darlin'. An' I was thinkin' I'd not set eyes on you again, me lovely."

Carrie stopped and stared at the man walking towards her across the stone-strewn floor of the abbey ruins. Her arms fell limply to her sides.

Lloyd Foster! Not Jamie.

Lloyd's arms were strong about her and if she had not been so disappointed because it was he and not Jamie, she might have welcomed the support and warmth he offered.

"Go away," she said weakly.

"Aw, now an' you don't mean that, to be sure."

Exhausted, scarcely able to think rationally, Carrie found herself leaning against him. This last disappointment had swept away the last reserve of her strength and left her helpless and without hope.

"Come on, me darlin'." He lifted her and carried her to his horse. "I'll not let anyone be hurtin' you ever again, do you hear dat now?"

She heard his words, soft, comforting words, but did not comprehend them. She just knew she was unable to resist him any longer. She could no longer stop him taking her home. She had no will, no strength left.

He sat her on his horse and mounted behind her. He took off his jacket and wrapped it round her and held her close, warming her cold, aching limbs. The rain soaked his fine waistcoat and shirt, but Lloyd Foster smiled. He had found her! She had not gone away with young Trent. He had found her in time. But his smile was tinged with sadness, for he knew that it was mere chance that she had not gone away with her lover, for it had been Jamie Trent she had been waiting for in the ruins. But now he had her again, Lloyd Foster did not intend to lose her this time.

As they rode down the hill towards the stream, he saw suddenly the line of men – farm labourers – advancing with slow and deliberate steps towards the workings of the embankment. Foster saw the makeshift weapons they carried and, afraid of their intention, he spurred his horse forward. The sudden movement stirred Carrie and she clung to him. "What is it?"

"I t'ink dere's trouble . . ."

He saw his navvies become aware of the advancing foe, saw them pick up their working tools and automatically form themselves into a line facing their attackers.

Carrie, now fully aroused, gasped in horror. As the two lines of men met, staves waved in the air, knife blades flashed and the cries of pain and triumph wafted to their ears.

Lloyd Foster leapt from his horse. "Stay here, me darlin' out of harm's way." Carrie narrowed her eyes, trying to see . . .

"*Luke*!" A horrified shriek escaped her lips. "Oh, look!"

Lloyd Foster ran towards the fight whilst Carrie watched with terrified eyes. She saw a huge fellow lunge towards her brother, saw him raise his crook and deal Luke a vicious blow, saw him fall to the ground, the man raising his weapon yet again. Then Foster reached him, grasped him by the collar and twisted him round. His huge fist smashed into the man's face, felling him at once. Then he picked Luke up in his arms and moved away from the fighting. Carrie scrambled from the horse and ran towards them. "Oh, Luke, *Luke*!"

But the young man was unconscious.

"We'll get him home."

"What – about the rest?"

Lloyd shrugged. "Dey'll have to fight it out, won't they now? And may the best men win!" He grinned at her, confident that victory would be with his navvies.

As Lloyd Foster lifted Luke gently from the horse outside the shack, Evan Smithson opened the door.

"There's a fight going on in Abbeyford. The farm labourers have attacked the navvies," Foster said curtly to him. "You should be there."

"Luke's in charge there ..." Evan began, then seeing the still form in Lloyd's strong arms, he gave a click of annoyance. "Can't he do anything? Oh," he added catching sight of Carrie, "you're back, are you?"

Carrie's answer was to push past him into the shack. Holding the door open she beckoned Lloyd to carry Luke inside and lay him down on the rough shakedown behind the ragged curtain.

"I'll be getting back to the trouble. You comin'?" he demanded of Evan.

"In a moment," Evan was looking down at his son thoughtfully. "You," he said to Carrie, pushing her roughly, "get some water. I'll be with you in a minute." It was a dismissal of both Carrie and Foster. Evan wanted them both out of the way.

Alone with his son, Evan knelt down by his side and felt amongst the boy's clothing. Something rustled, and Evan drew out a crumpled piece of paper.

As Carrie returned with a bowl of water and rags to bind Luke's head, she saw her father rising from a crouching position beside Luke, his hand inside his own coat pocket. As he stood and turned to leave, she saw the gleam of triumph in his eyes.

"He's all yours now – but I doubt you'll be able to do aught with him!" His tone was unemotional, as one might speak of an injured animal, not a human being, not his own son!

Evan brushed past her and was gone. Carrie stood a moment, wondering at his strange actions, then, as a low moan came from Luke's lips, all other thoughts were driven from her mind save the care of her brother. She knelt and began to bathe his wounds.

On the other side of the curtain, seated at the table, Lucy sat motionless staring into space, totally resigned to face the loss of yet another of her offspring.

The fight was over and the navvies had won. The village men returned battered and beaten to their homes. Two were dead and three more seriously injured, and not one of them survived without a wound of some sort. The victorious navvies began two days of heavy drinking ending with a march through Abbeyford village, where they took their revenge by smashing property and fighting anyone and everyone, young or old, who got in their way.

Then they returned to work on building their railway as if nothing had happened! But the bitterness and hatred in the village was irreparable.

Carrie nursed Luke devotedly, pushing all thoughts of her own happiness aside as she tried to save the life of her brother. But her knowledge of nursing was scant, and her brother too ill with consumption anyway to survive for many more years. His wound had merely precipitated the inevitable!

For two days he lay on the shakedown, sometimes unconscious, sometimes mumbling incoherently.

"Beautiful lady. Never seen – anyone so – before."

"Letter – the letter. Carrie!"

"Not strong, can't fight him. Ruin us all . . . The letter – give . . ."

Carrie listened and heard but could not understand everything. Obviously his wandering mind was remembering Francesca, the lovely girl he had seen with Lady Lynwood. But the murmurings about a letter she could not understand.

On the third day after the fight, Luke died, quite quietly and quickly.

Carrie shed a few tears, but her mother, Lucy, was beyond tears, her emotions all used up over the harsh years of continual grief. Evan was unmoved, and the only comfort Carrie received came from Lloyd Foster.

Luke was buried in Abbeyford churchyard, so hurriedly it was almost indecent, Carrie thought. Several of the villagers gathered but only to stare with hostility at the three figures near the grave – Evan Smithson, Carrie and Lloyd Foster.

As they left the churchyard, Foster drew her arm through his own and patted her hand. "Carrie, me lovely, you know I want you to be me wife. I've a special licence here," he patted his coat pocket. "Been carrying it around next me heart these past few weeks now, so I have. I have a mind to go abroad – to build railways in far-off lands, an' I want you to be with me. Do you hear me now?" His voice was gentle, coaxing, quite unlike the brash Irishman she had always thought him.

"Oh, Lloyd, I owe you so much. You tried to save Luke's life from that – that mob," she glanced fearfully behind her to see the surly eyes of the villagers still upon them. "But – but I don't – I can't love you, you know that."

Again he patted her hand and sighed heavily. "I know, I know. But, me darlin', he's gone. Your pa told me. An' if you come with me, I'll be good to you – I swear it on your brother's grave, so I do." She glanced up at him and his eyes were on her, serious and full of love.

"Oh, Lloyd – I'm sorry, I can't."

But Carrie had reckoned without the determination of her father. "He's gone. Left you. His sort won't *marry* the likes of you. 'Specially now he's found out you're a blood relative!"

His words were like a knife in her heart, robbing her of all the belief she had held of Jamie's love for her. Her last memory of him had been as he had rushed past her and ridden off, ignoring her cry of desperation.

Somehow she found herself, as if in a dream, as if the events were happening around her and she had no will, no power to prevent them, agreeing to marry Lloyd Foster.

The marriage was performed – like Luke's funeral – hurriedly, early in the morning with only her father and mother present, besides Lloyd Foster and herself. Lloyd was dressed in his fine clothes whilst the bride stood, a pathetic, unhappy creature in her ragged skirt and shawl, making her promises in a mechanical tone.

As they came out of the church, far above them, unnoticed by any of them, a rider sat on his horse beside the ruined wall of the abbey.

Jamie Trent narrowed his eyes and though the distance was too great to recognise the tiny figures moving away from the church, somehow in his heart he knew their identity. He had returned that morning, riding through the night and going straight to the abbey ruins with the vain hope of finding Carrie waiting for him. He knew that, if she wanted to see him, that was where she would be waiting.

He watched, motionless, his eyes following the group of figures as they moved along the lane, lost from sight for a time amongst the hedgerows and then appearing again as they climbed the hill out of Abbeyford.

Jamie closed his eyes and groaned aloud and then turned his horse towards the Manor.

In the stable, hanging by the neck from a rope round a beam was the stiff, cold body of Squire Guy Trent. Jamie leaned his head against the rough wood of the door and gave way to total despair.

Foster could hardly get Carrie away from Abbeyford quickly enough. The Railway Board had accepted Evan as the new contractor, and with the marriage between Foster and Carrie, the private bargain struck between Evan Smithson and Lloyd Foster was complete. Carrie had no belongings to pack and so, only hours after their wedding, they were climbing into a pony and trap after a brief farewell to her mother and younger brothers and moving off down the rough cart-track to start a new life. Evan Smithson watched them go, his arms folded across his chest, a smile of satisfaction on his face.

Now for the railway!

As the trap rattled along the lane, suddenly a man stepped out into their path a little way ahead. Lloyd Foster pulled hard on the reins and brought the vehicle to a standstill.

'Jamie!" Carrie whispered. Then she turned pleading eyes upon Lloyd. "Please – let me – speak to him? Just – for a moment."

Lloyd hesitated and then sadly nodded his head in agreement, his heart heavy as she scrambled down so eagerly from her seat beside him and ran towards Jamie Trent. He did not reach out his arms towards her and his stillness stopped her flinging herself against him.

"Jamie?" There was uncertainty in her tone, but only for a moment, for then she saw the wealth of misery in his eyes, which matched the ache in her own heart. He loved her still! He had come back for her – but too late!

"I thought you'd gone – for good," she whispered.

Jamie shook his head, and his voice when he spoke was low and hoarse with emotion. "No – no. I went to Manchester to see the lawyers. To see if I could save my land."

"And – did you?"

He shook his head. "And I lost something far more precious in my absence. Oh, Carrie," he reached out and touched her cheek with his fingertips. "Why did you not believe in me? Didn't my letter convince you . . .?"

"Letter?" Carrie's voice was shrill. "What letter?"

"I left a letter with Luke telling you where I'd gone. Telling you I'd be back for you."

Carrie closed her eyes and groaned. "Oh, no, *no*! Jamie – Luke's dead. He was hurt. There was a fight between your farmworkers and the navvies. Lloyd," she gestured with her hand behind her towards the man sitting so silent and still in the trap, unable to hear their words and yet torn with jealousy to see them together, "tried to save him, but he died three days after. Jamie, he murmured about a letter – I couldn't understand. And there was no letter on him, I know . . ."

Grim-faced, Jamie said bitterly, "Your father must have found it."

Carrie gasped and the picture of Evan Smithson bending over Luke's still form as she had returned to tend his wounds flashed across her mind, his hand, as he stood up and turned towards her, inside his own coat pocket. In that moment Carrie hated her father.

"So, he's got what he wanted," Jamie said. "My land, Grandfather's death – and you married to Foster!"

"Your grandfather?"

Jamie's head dropped. "Yes – I found him this morning. He must have been dead a – couple of days. He – he'd killed himself."

"Oh, Jamie," Carrie whispered, horrified. "I'm so sorry."

There was nothing left to say. Their emotions were too deep for words. Gently, Jamie took her arm, turned her round and led her back to Lloyd Foster.

As Jamie helped Carrie into the trap the two men's eyes met. There was no animosity between them, more a look of understanding and mutual pity, for whilst one had lost her, the other had not won her love. There was an unspoken request in Jamie's eyes. 'Take care of her, be good to her', and an answering promise in Lloyd Foster's, yet not a word was spoken.

Lloyd Foster slapped the reins and the trap jerked forward. Twisting round, Carrie watched Jamie's figure grow smaller and smaller as she was carried away from him.

Just once, he raised his hand in a final farewell.

Chapter Five

They travelled for several days, stopping at wayside inns, making for London.

That first night, their wedding night, she sat in the bedroom, tense and fearful, waiting for him to come to her. She sat by the window, shivering and staring out into the darkness, seeing nothing, but determined to stay as far away from the big double bed as she could. She kept her eyes averted from it, trembling at the thought of what she must endure.

Carrie was no maiden, afraid of the unknown. Her fear lay only in that, having known the joys of loving with Jamie, she must now submit to the passions of a man she did not love.

They had been welcomed into the inn by the beaming landlord, who, though she could see the question in his eyes, politely ignored the incongruity of a well-dressed gentleman accompanied by a gypsy girl.

"I'll be wantin' a *double* room," Lloyd Foster had said firmly, and Carrie had felt a twinge of revulsion at the thought of what was to happen that night. "An' mind the bed is clean and warm for my wife, an' a fire in the grate."

"Of course, sir. Mary Ellen," the landlord had shouted to one of the kitchen maids, "away and prepare the room, girl – the *best* front bedroom." He had turned back to Lloyd. "And you'll be wanting refreshment, sir, I don't doubt. Now we have a nice roast veal, and some of the best wine this side the Channel, sir."

Bowing, he had ushered Lloyd and Carrie to high-backed bench seats in a secluded corner. Two brass candlesticks with lighted candles stood on the table. They sat opposite each other and waited for their meal to be served. Carrie's violet eyes were dark, the soft candlelight highlighting her beauty, but she was unaware of her own appearance. All her senses prickled at the nearness of the man sitting so close, his knees accidentally touching hers beneath the table. Though the meal was such as she had never tasted before – tender veal, sparkling wine which tickled her nose as she raised the glass to her lips, a sweet of delicious meringue and fresh cream, and coffee, real, steaming hot coffee, fresh and fragrant – Carrie could not enjoy it. She felt as if she could never enjoy life itself again.

Now, as she sat in the bedroom, she felt such a loneliness that she had never before known. Always, she had fought for survival. She had been the strength her weaker brothers – and even her mother – had leaned on. And now, plucked from their midst, even with the promise of security and comfort, she felt bereft. Torn away from all she knew, all that was familiar and – worst of all – torn from the very first man with whom she had fallen in love . . .

The bedroom door opened with a scrape and she jumped and turned to see Lloyd Foster standing in the doorway. He came in and closed the door behind him and stood looking at her. The silence between them lengthened until it grated on her nerves. She turned back to gazing out of the window, even though she could see nothing through the blackness. She was acutely aware of him standing behind her. She felt a shiver down her spine as he crossed the room and moved close to her.

He reached out and touched her shoulder and she flinched from his touch. He sprang away as if burned. "So, that is how it is to be, is it?" His voice was low with emotion. "Rough I may be, but I'm no ignorant brute. But you're my wife, and, by God, you'll be my wife!"

Gone was his joviality. There was no mistaking the steel in his voice. Carrie shuddered. She had heard it before, but never directed at herself until this moment. He turned and strode from the room, banging the door behind him. As she heard his feet clatter down the stairs, Carrie could only feel relief.

Lloyd Foster made his way to the saloon bar, where he drank steadily through the night until drunkenness dulled his frustrated passion for his bride.

The following day, much to Carrie's surprise, Lloyd Foster seemed to have recovered his usual cheerful spirits. He laughed loudly with the innkeeper, tipped the stable boy lavishly for looking after the horse and was courteous towards Carrie. She avoided meeting his gaze and so did not see for herself the pain deep in his eyes, hidden by his outward show of good humour. She was quiet, withdrawn into her own private misery, repulsing all attempts Foster made to reach her.

They travelled on, Carrie sullen and silent, Foster singing Irish folksongs at the top of his loud and surprisingly tuneful voice. They stayed in a pleasant hotel in London, though where Foster slept Carrie never knew nor cared to enquire, for each night she slept alone.

He took her to the shops and insisted she should buy herself a trousseau, but Carrie had no idea how a lady should dress and was at the mercy of the dressmaker. All manner of clothing was laid before her, such items as she had never seen, let alone possessed. Flannel vests, cotton chemises, petticoats, corsets, cotton drawers, white thread stockings, coloured silk stockings, kid gloves, silk gloves, morning dresses and afternoon dresses of silk cashmere, black silk skirts and bodices, two evening gowns and a white lace ball gown, so beautiful it took Carrie's breath away. Shawls and cloaks and hats, even a parasol edged with lace. Neat button boots and shoes for day and evening wear which Carrie's feet had never known.

"I can't accept all this," she hissed at Lloyd Foster, gesturing towards all the garments being wrapped by the willing assistants.

"Ah, so you can find it in you to speak to me," Lloyd said, his mouth smiling but his eyes reproachful. It was the first time she had spoken to him since their marriage – except to answer his questions in sullen monosyllables. "And you will accept it. It is a husband's duty to provide for his wife, is it not, now?"

Her violet eyes flashed – the first time she had shown any spark of life since leaving Abbeyford.

"I'll not be *bought*!" She glared at him, standing facing him in the centre of the fashionable shop, her hands on her hips.

"Oh, an' I love you when you're angry," Lloyd Foster's booming laugh rang out, causing the dressmaker to 'tut-tut' and her young assistants to giggle to each other. Carrie stamped her foot, causing the girls to give little shrieks of horror. It was the behaviour they were not accustomed to seeing in their shop – not the behaviour of a lady!

"*I'm* serious – even if you're not," Carrie cried angrily.

"Oh, me darlin', I was never more serious in the whole of me life." The hint of steel was in his eyes again. He took hold of her wrist, and though he only held her lightly with one hand, she could feel the strength in his fingers. "You will accept these gifts, my lovely *wife*!" The accent on the last word was audible only to Carrie.

Thwarted, she flounced out of the shop and stood waiting for him in the street outside. He sauntered out in due course, now seeming quite unperturbed by her outburst.

As they walked along she stole a glance at him. Wherever he was, she thought, he seemed at ease. Whether it was amongst the navvies, covered with dust, or with Squire Trent playing cards, or here in the fashionable quarter of London, he was equally at home and – amazingly – accepted. Whilst she felt a misfit, a dirty, dishevelled gypsy with no manners and no idea of etiquette.

She was quiet now and as they walked along she looked about her at the shops, at the grand carriages, at the coachmen and footmen in their smart liveried uniforms, and at the noblemen and fashionable ladies inside the carriages. Lloyd walked at her side, smartly dressed as ever in a well-cut suit, a brightly coloured waistcoat, his watch-chain looped across his broad chest, and swinging a cane.

Suddenly he reached down and took her hand and drew it through his arm. She could feel the curious glances of the passers-by and the colour rose in her cheeks.

"You see, me darlin'," Lloyd was saying in his lilting brogue. "I want to see you dressed in fine silks and satins. You've the beauty of a fine lady already, me darlin', all you're needin' is the fine feathers. Do y'hear me now? There's so many places I can take you. Now, wouldn't you like to play the fine lady?"

Carrie was silent.

She supposed she should feel gratitude to him for his generosity, but she could not forgive him for having aided her father in tricking her into this marriage, tearing her from the arms of her lover. But as the days passed into weeks and months, she found she could not help being caught up in the excited bustle of the vast city. The shops fascinated her, the fancy carriages, the beautifully dressed ladies in the silks and velvets. She even had a maid of her very own now – a young girl who helped her dress her hair and bedeck herself in her new finery.

Away from Abbeyford, away from all the squalor and hardship of her former life, away from the anguish of losing her brother, Luke, of seeing her mother weary and beaten, away from her brutish, obsessed father and with so much that was new to interest her, she found the pain begin to lessen and her natural vitality slowly reassert itself.

Carrie Smithson Foster was a survivor. She was strong and blessed with a natural zest for life that could not, would not, be beaten or bowed for long.

In the company of Lloyd Foster's jovial spirit, she could not remain locked in her private misery for ever, so resolutely she raised her head, accepted his gifts and determined to make the best of the situation. She could not forgive him or give herself to him willingly – but between them, on the surface at least, there was an uneasy kind of truce.

Carrie still slept alone and never troubled to enquire where, or how, her husband spent his nights.

Lloyd was true to his promise. He introduced her to a life she had never dreamed existed. True it was not the life of aristocratic Society – those doors were closed even to Lloyd Foster. But they found their niche amongst the middle-class, well-to-do, 'respectable'

Victorians. Carrie began to enjoy her new role, laughing secretly at the thought of the astonishment on the faces of these fine ladies if they knew of her past life – her impoverished childhood and harsh living. Now she mimicked their manner of speaking, their elegant way of walking, their affectations, yet she never lost her earthy honesty, her strength of will.

Yet, deep in her heart, she was lonely for sight of Jamie. *Gladly she would have forsaken all this luxury – and more – for one kiss from her lover.*

"Now, you sit here at this table, me darlin', and I'll be fetchin' you some ginger beer."

Carrie sat down at the table in the tea-garden to which Lloyd had brought her. It was April, over four months since she had left Abbeyford – and Jamie. Amidst the hustle of the tea-garden, Carrie felt the loneliness steal over her. She looked about her at the happy families – mothers in their beribboned bonnets, their wide crinolines spread about them, leaning down to tend their small children. The gentlemen in their pink shirts and blue waistcoats seemed to gravitate to one corner of the garden, where they smoked their cigars and leant on their canes, with their tall silk hats at a rakish angle.

"Here we are, me darlin'," Lloyd placed a glass of ginger beer on the table before her and a dish of winkles. "Now – you'll be all right for a moment, I just have a little business to attend to," and, weaving his way between the tables, avoiding two boys chasing each other across the grass, Lloyd went to join the other gentlemen.

Carrie saw them greet him like a friend – he was obviously known to three or four of them.

It was a huge place where they were, on the banks of the river Thames. Far in one corner, Carrie could see a crowd clustering round a balloonist who was making ready to begin his ascent. She did not join the crowd but watched with casual interest from where she was sitting. The spring day was surprisingly warm here in the sheltered tea-garden. In her wide-skirted crinoline with its numerous petticoats and the close-fitting bonnet beneath which her hair was arranged into a neat chignon, she felt uncomfortably restricted and hot. In that moment she longed for the freedom she had known last summer, her black hair flying loose, her bare feet running through the long grass to the abbey ruins to meet Jamie.

Tears prickled her eyelids and she sighed. Now it could never be. She was here in London, dressed in fine clothes, trying to ape the lady, married to a man she hated.

But did she really *hate* him? Carrie turned her gaze to where her husband stood. At that moment he threw back his head and laughed at something one of the other men had said, a loud, infectious sound that caused those nearby to smile too.

He was certainly a fine figure of a man, a man any woman could be proud to marry – any woman but Carrie, whose heart belonged to another!

She turned her eyes away again and watched the balloonist as he rose, a little jerkily at first, above the ground. The crowd 'oh'ed' and 'ah'ed' and then he was soaring above their heads and drifting away from them across the Thames.

You are married to Lloyd Foster, Carrie told herself sharply. He treats you well and your life is more comfortable and luxurious than you had ever believed possible for the gypsy Carrie Smithson. You had better make the best of it! But her heart longed for Jamie to see her dressed in fine clothes. How much more worthy of being *his* wife she was now than she had been a year ago.

That evening, back in their hotel room, Lloyd suddenly said, "Now, me darlin', how would you like to be goin' to Paris?"

Carrie swung round to face him, unable for once to prevent him seeing the joy shining in her eyes. "Paris? Do you mean it?"

"Now would I be jokin' about a t'ing like that?"

She put her head on one side and regarded him thoughtfully. "We'll be coming back, won't we?"

Lloyd Foster avoided her gaze. "Ah, well, now, an' that's a little difficult to be sayin'. You see, I've got to earn a livin' for us, haven't I now?"

Carrie's mouth tightened. "I thought you'd made your fortune at the expense of others. Twisting people out of their inheritance by taking advantage of a drunkard seems to be your way!"

It was the first time they had spoken of it, although always it lay like a barrier between them.

"I'll not suffer your reproaches the rest of our lives," he growled. Carrie said nothing and the silence between them grew as they glared at each other, challenging. Suddenly, as if unable to bear it any longer, Lloyd strode towards her and took her in his arms. His mouth was upon hers, his hands tearing at her clothing. For a moment she struggled, but he was too strong for her. He took her, not brutally as she had feared, but demandingly, possessively.

"You are *mine*," he muttered against her cheek, "all mine. God knows how I've waited this long!"

Afterwards he left her abruptly without another word. She lay in the double bed, her emotions in a turmoil. She knew now what it must have cost Lloyd Foster these past months to stay away from her bed. Since that tentative approach the very first night when she had cringed from him he had never again made any attempt to touch her. Not until now.

Now, finally, as they had quarrelled openly his passions had boiled over and he could no longer hold back.

"Possess my body he may," she promised herself, "but my heart – never! He took me away from Jamie," she told herself fiercely. But Lloyd is your husband, her conscience reminded her, and he has been good to you.

In Paris they stayed in a fine hotel. Lloyd took her dining in the best restaurants and courted her with gifts. "Didn't I say you'd be the fine lady, me darlin'? You're every bit as lovely as these Society ladies, so you are."

Paris was a truly romantic city. Carrie was caught up in the whirl of the life there. Everything she saw she committed to memory and learnt from it, so swiftly that soon she was able to move in the middle-class society with ease as if she had been born into such circles and not bred in a mud hut, with bare feet and scarcely a wrap to keep her warm in winter!

She heard no news from England. Not of her family, nor of Jamie Trent. Though Lloyd came to her often now, many nights she still slept alone. Occasionally, she wondered where her husband went when he was not by her side.

He took her through France and, as winter encroached, they moved south until they reached Cannes.

Cannes was fast becoming a place where it was fashionable for the wealthy British to buy a piece of land and build a villa. Then when the English winter became too chill they could travel to their 'winter resort' on the Mediterranean coast.

"Do you know," Lloyd pointed out the villas to her as they drove by in a hired carriage. "Do you know that they even have turf shipped from England – renewed every year if they need it. Can you imagine a fellow bein' rich enough to be able to do that?"

Carrie looked at the magnificent villas, white and shining in the sun, surrounded by groves of orange and lemon trees. "No," she said soberly, "I *cannot* imagine it!"

Lloyd laughed and put his arm about her slim waist. "Ah, me darlin', we'll be rich one day. You'll have everything you ever dreamed of!"

Carrie glanced down at the green silk crinoline she wore, at the fine gloves, at her feet encased in satin slippers. Already she owned more than she had ever thought possible. But how swiftly she would abandon it all to be back in her coarse skirt and bare feet, to be back in the abbey ruins in Jamie's arms. *That* was all she had dreamed of!

Lloyd rented a villa and they stayed in Cannes. Almost against her will, Carrie grew to love the pretty town nestling in a bay, the beautiful blue sea, the mountains. She blossomed in the warmth of the sun and in the clear air. Her thinness was gone, the pale, half-starved look. Her skin glowed with health and she matured from a young, passionate – yet undernourished – girl into a beautiful woman, serene yet somehow remote. Always, deep in her violet eyes there was a sadness.

"You know what dey'll be wantin' here, all these wealthy Englishmen, is a railway – a passenger railway from Paris to the south coast," Lloyd said standing on the balcony of the villa overlooking the blue sea. He glanced back into the bedroom where

Carrie was lying on the bed, fanning her face vigorously. It was the first time the word 'railway' had been mentioned between them.

"Really," Carrie's tone was non-committal, bored almost, as she flapped at an intruding mosquito.

"There's only about four hundred miles of railway in the whole of France," he was saying, suppressed excitement in his voice. "And that's mainly for the carrying of coal."

"Really," Carrie said again and closed her eyes, not noticing the expression on Lloyd's face as he looked at her and sighed and then went back to gazing out to sea.

This life of high-living was all very well, he was thinking, but I'm beginning to miss me railways. He couldn't push the matter too far – not yet. He must give Carrie time to forget. But, some day, somehow, somewhere, he knew he must once again build a railway.

It was in his blood!

As the months stretched into years Lloyd Foster grew increasingly restless. Between himself and Carrie the uneasy truce remained. She was his wife in every sense now and yet always there was a shadow between them, the shadow of her love for another man and of Abbeyford and all its memories.

"We'll have to go back to Paris," Lloyd told her. "That's the centre of things. We've been here in Cannes three years and I'm missing what's happening. Louis Philippe passed an Act in 1842 for the construction of a great network of trunk routes from Paris over the whole of France. I could be part of all that. Damn it – I *want* to be part of it!"

So back they went to Paris. Unfortunately for Lloyd, things did not work out as he wanted. For another two years he tried to find employment as a railway builder, but once again there was confusion in Paris and although a network of railways had been approved in theory, the actual construction was a different matter. Economic difficulties in France and the air of unrest, which at any moment might erupt into revolution yet again, made investors wary and the capital required for the railways was not forthcoming.

"Damn it all!" Lloyd burst out, striding up and down the hotel bedroom whilst Carrie sat at the dressing-table, arranging her hair in readiness for a ball they were to attend. "There's nothing here for me. The whole city is in a turmoil! They're never at peace, these people! Now, they're wanting to be rid of Louis Philippe!" He paused a moment and then said, "They're so wrapped up in their political intrigues, there's going to be no progress for the next year or so. There's no railways for me to build *here*! We'll have to look elsewhere. I must find work!" And he punched one clenched fist into the palm of his other hand.

Carrie stopped brushing her hair, her brush suspended in mid-air, and turned to look at him, suddenly interested. "You mean you've come to the end of your 'fortune'?"

Lloyd's laughter filled the room. "Me darlin', there never was a 'fortune'. How do you think I've made us a livin' these past five years, eh?"

Carrie shrugged. "I thought it was the money you'd made building railways in England. You always seemed a wealthy man."

Again he laughed. "Ah, me darlin', there's still much you don't know about me. Where do you think I spend me nights when I'm not beside you?"

"I neither know nor care."

The pain was fleetingly in his eyes, then he said. "For your information, madam, the money which buys you all these fine fripperies," his fingers touched the lace on her white shoulder, "comes from gambling."

She swivelled round quickly on the stool to stare at him in amazement. "*Gambling*?"

"Aye, whilst you're sleepin', I've been playing at card-tables here and in Cannes, earning us a livin'."

"Well!" Carrie was speechless. "*Well*!" was all she could say again.

"But I'm tired of it now. I've had enough of the high livin', the drinkin' and gamblin'. I want to get back to railways."

Carrie's lips parted and her eyes shone. "If there's nothing here, then – then – we're going home? Back to England?"

Lloyd's eyes darkened with anger, his mouth became hard. "No, I don't mean dat at all," he said harshly, her joyful anticipation bringing back all the antagonism between them. "We're *never* going back to England, d'ye hear me?"

As the look of hope died in her eyes now, Lloyd's tone softened a little. "I've met this man, a captain in the British Army in India. Stationed at Calcutta, he is. He's been on furlough – enjoying himself in Paris," he grinned. "Well – he tells me they're planning to build a railway from Calcutta. There's a lot of wrangling goin' on, so it seems, but I've got used to that this past two years in Paris. He reckons if I was to get out there, maybe have a look at terrain, I could persuade the powers that be to hurry things along a little, y'know. Captain Richmond'll be at the ball tonight. Now, ye'll be nice to him, won't you, for my sake?"

Carrie turned back to the mirror and resumed brushing her hair with sharp, angry strokes. "India! That's the other side of the world. I don't want to go. I *won't* go!"

"Well, me darlin', we're going!"

"This is Captain Richmond," Lloyd introduced a gentleman in military uniform to Carrie.

"I'm happy to make your acquaintance, ma'am." The Captain took her hand in his, bent over it with a show of gallantry and raised it to his lips. As he lifted his head, his eyes looked into her face with bold audacity.

"Captain," she murmured.

He was undeniably handsome. Tall and slim, with fair hair, bright blue eyes and a small, neat moustache. He was indeed resplendent in his scarlet coat, with its white sash across the chest, the gold braiding and shining gold buttons. He was elegant and his whole manner and bearing exuded confidence – the kind of self-assurance that only comes from having been born into a wealthy family, of accepting the place in life as a leader of men as one's natural right.

"May I have the pleasure of this next dance, ma'am?" Carrie inclined her head and she moved gracefully on to the dance floor on his arm.

"You dance exquisitely, Mrs Foster."

She smiled at his compliment. How his face would alter, she thought mischievously, if he knew my background and my upbringing.

"I was fortunate enough to learn to dance here, in Paris," she told him.

"Ah, then that explains it."

They danced for a short time in silence, then the Captain said, "Your husband is a delightful fellow. Unique, one might say. I've played cards with him several times and don't he have the devil's own luck ...?" He paused as the steps of the dance took them apart. "He never seems to lose!"

"Really," Carrie said with an air of complete uninterest.

"But, then," the Captain smiled, his blue eyes intent upon her, "perhaps it's the charm of all his Irish blarney. Is that how he came to capture such a prize as yourself, ma'am?

The smile died on Carrie's lips, her violet eyes were dark with sudden misery and her steps faltered in the dance, causing her to miss a sequence. His question had evoked unhappy memories. The Captain seemed faintly amused. "Forgive my audacity, ma'am, but amongst these fair, milk-white maidens your dark beauty is so striking. Your eyes are like the spring violets ..."

"Pray, sir, your compliments are extreme!" Carrie, once more in control of her emotions, smiled.

His eyes were upon her face, his smooth voice low and intense. "Indeed they are not, ma'am, I assure you!"

The dance ended and he led her back to where Lloyd Foster waited.

Captain Richmond was the epitome of politeness, yet in his eyes there was danger when his gaze rested on Carrie. If it were not for the protective presence of the huge figure of her husband, Carrie thought, I should have need to fear this man. She put her arm through Lloyd's and smiled up at Captain Richmond, believing herself secure in the thought that a man of such good breeding would not encroach upon another man's preserves.

"Have you decided, Foster?" Captain Richmond addressed her husband but his gaze never strayed from Carrie for long.

"Well, now, I'm thinking I've nothing to lose by comin' out to India. Me only concern is for me lovely wife here. Will it be possible to find a comfortable place for her, d'ya think? Havin' never been to India, I just don't know what to expect. D'you understand me now?"

"Indeed I do," the Captain smiled. "There are many European inhabitants in Calcutta, wealthy merchants and the like. We should have no trouble in finding suitable accommodation for your good lady," he gave a slight bow in Carrie's direction and added, almost as an afterthought, "and for yourself."

At that moment another gentleman requested Carrie to dance and she left her husband and the Captain eagerly planning the proposed trip to India. Carrie sighed inwardly. Lloyd had become animated at the thought of being once more involved with the building of a railway. After all the disappointments he had met here in Paris these last two years, now his hopes were rekindled.

She guessed his self-imposed exile from the work he so obviously loved had been entirely on her account. He had wanted to remove her from the environment of railway building that would always remind her of Abbeyford – and of Jamie! But now, after five years of living off his wits and his dexterity at cards, the man hungered for useful, constructive work once more.

The dance ended and as the young dandy led her back across the floor to her husband and she saw his eyes seek out her face, for the first time since her marriage she felt a flash of genuine fondness for him.

If only, she thought half-regretfully, I had not already given my heart so irrevocably to another, maybe I could have found real happiness with Lloyd Foster.

The ship was moving, under the direction of the Pilot, the last forty or so miles through the Ganges delta towards Calcutta on the east bank of the river Hooghly. Carrie stood on deck between her husband and Captain Richmond. The three months which this voyage had taken, throwing the three of them into close proximity, had rendered a subtle change in the relationship between them. Carrie had, with each day that passed, come to fear Captain Richmond a little more, and in so doing had drawn closer to Lloyd for security. Her husband had seen nothing amiss and the Captain was careful not to let him see the lust which flashed in his eyes when he looked at Carrie, but she had seen it! Lloyd did not feel the underlying challenge in Jeremy Richmond's mocking tone. He accepted the Captain as a man who would introduce him to the right people in India, on whom his future depended. So Carrie remained silent.

"Will yer look at dose swamps?" Lloyd was saying. Carrie saw the treacherous swamps, with palms and mangroves and sticky mud. Birds rose from the trees and they could hear the sounds of the undergrowth. She shuddered. "I don't like it," she murmured. "It's so hot and – *eerie!*"

"Not many dare to venture in there, Mrs Foster," Captain Richmond glanced down at her. "There's all manner of snakes, tigers, monkeys – to say nothing of the crocodiles!"

Carrie glanced down over the side of the boat, as if fearful of seeing one of the monsters sliding by. She looked up again towards the bank, and then cried out in surprise. "Why, there's a village. I thought you said the place was uninhabited?"

"That's a *native* village, ma'am." His tone was condescending and Carrie pursed her lips.

"They're people, none the less," she replied sharply.

"A little farther on you will see a clearing where a European indigo planter has his bungalow and factory, and later still an area called Garden Reach, where rich European merchants and officials have their homes. It's quite the 'little England'," Captain Richmond added, his tone heavy with sarcasm.

Eventually, Carrie saw the place he mentioned – houses with verandahs and flower-beds and trees. She could see children running on the well-kept lawns with their ayahs – their Indian nursemaids. There were even one or two pet dogs barking playfully.

Then as they rounded the final curve Carrie's attention was

caught by the busy harbour. It seemed crammed with boats of all descriptions – barges, fishing-boats, clippers, and all manner of small boats. Set high above were the ramparts of Fort William.

"Will that be where you are stationed, Captain?" Lloyd asked.

"It is indeed, sir," was the reply.

Carrie saw that amongst the Indian coolies on the dock side, amidst the bustle of bullock carts, camel carts and barrows, stood a few British or European people, men in top hats and women in fine crinolines. There were even a few British landaus pulled by shining horses. Behind the teeming dockside, rose a skyline of magnificent towers and domes.

After they had left the ship, Captain Richmond found lodgings for them in the Garden Reach district.

"This house belongs to – er – a friend of mine. He is away at present, but I know he would not mind you having the use of it."

"We are most grateful to you, Captain, to be sure," Lloyd laughed and slapped his new-found friend upon the shoulder, but the Captain's gaze was upon Carrie as if it were her gratitude alone he sought.

"Pray make yourselves comfortable," he said, bowing, his insolent gaze never leaving her face. "There are servants to do your bidding. I must report to Fort William, but I shall return tomorrow to see that you have all you need."

Carrie inclined her head, but she could not bring herself to enthuse over the Captain's seeming kindness. She felt instinctively that one day, somehow, he would demand repayment.

Her husband made up for Carrie's lack of gratitude. "I don't know what we should have done without the Captain, me darlin', in this strange land."

"But for the Captain, we should not *be* in this strange land!" Carrie retorted sharply and flounced out of the room.

That night Carrie lay in a huge bed under a mosquito curtain. England seemed so very far away now. She had had no word from her family since her marriage. Nor had she had any news of Jamie. Was he still in Abbeyford? Was he married, with children? Though her homeland and family were far removed, Jamie's face was still vivid in her recollection. His face was before her, tender, loving, and then finally filled with the desperate misery of their final parting.

Lloyd Foster lay a few feet from her in his own bed, flapping occasionally at a stray mosquito which had found its way in, but Carrie's thoughts were many hundreds of miles away. They had left England in the early spring – now it would be high summer there. She fell asleep dreaming of that wonderful summer when she had fallen in love ...

Chapter Six

For the next few months Lloyd Foster seemed rejuvenated. He would return to the house bursting with news, his enthusiasm spilling over. "Ah, Carrie me darlin', such opportunities here. Such visions. Oh, 'tis hard work there's ahead of us, to be sure. There's so much that's new."

"New? How?" Carrie asked, attempting to show interest though she found her days dull. Now that she had a houseful of barefoot servants, silently padding about their tasks, she found the days empty.

" 'Tis different to railway building in England. The climate is so different, the heat, the rains, to say nothing of the river changing its course before we get the bridges built!" He laughed. "And you should see the length they'll have to be." He spread his arms wide. "The rivers swell so, that the bridges have to be much, much longer than in England."

England! Carrie felt a great yearning sweep over her. But it was no use. Her husband was happy now he was once more going to build a railway – so here she must stay!

The months passed and Carrie found her days filled only with the social life of the European wives resident in Calcutta – tea-parties and afternoon visits; dinner-parties and balls.

There were delays with the actual beginning of the railway construction – and Lloyd began to chafe.

"I t'ought they was all ready to begin building and what do I find now?" He flung his arms wide in a gesture of despair. "I find there's two, if not three, different companies going to build different parts of the railway." He ticked them off on his fingers. "There's the Great India Peninsula Railway going to be built from Bombay; the East India Railway from Calcutta, to say nothing of a third company – the Madras Railway."

"Well, since we are in Calcutta, I suppose it's the East Indian Railway you're involved with, is that right?" Carrie asked reasonably.

"Yes, but . . ."

"And where is the line from Calcutta going exactly?"

"Supposed to be westwards over the Ganges plain to Lahore, but . . ."

"Then where," asked his wife calmly, in contrast to Lloyd, who was visibly heated, "is the difficulty?"

He paced the room. "Oh, 'tis all politics and guarantees and contracts and shareholders – just what I came here to try and escape. The East India Company were on the point of signing contracts with both the East India Railway and the Great India Peninsula Railway – and *now* what do they tell me?"

"I have no idea. What?" Carrie asked patiently.

"There's been some sort of financial crisis in Britain and revolutions in Europe and the companies cannot find the deposit required before signing the contracts. Then rival companies leap in and investors lose confidence in ours and so," he shrugged his shoulders, "it looks like another holdup. Oh, I don't understand it all – 'tis all high finance at government level – I only had to deal with directors of railway boards in England – an' I could handle them, but here . . . 'tis out of me hands." He sat down looking dejected and beaten.

"Do – do you think Captain Richmond knew this when he suggested you should come here?" she asked carefully.

Lloyd shook his head. "I don't suppose so. I reckon he's genuine enough."

Carrie said nothing, but she did not agree with him. She watched Lloyd. Her heart leapt. Perhaps he would be obliged to leave India, to go home, back to England. They had come here to build railways and if there was no railway to build . . .

But the irrepressible Irishman would not be deflated for long.

Before Carrie could utter any suggestion of her own, he had bounded to his feet again and, his hand on the door, turned to her to say briefly, "But, in the meantime, while all the wrangling goes on, there's no reason why I can't be surveying the land and makin' out me own case, now is there?"

He was gone, once more bounding with enthusiasm and energy.

Carrie sighed. It looked as if she must resign herself to life in India for a while yet.

The months stretched to a year before the contracts were at last signed and work could begin. Lloyd rubbed his hands. "We're to site the eastern terminal of the railway at Howrah on the west bank of the river Hooghly," he told Carrie.

"Really? Why not in Calcutta itself?"

"It would need an immense bridge from Calcutta across the river – it's over seventeen hundred feet wide there, even though that's its narrowest point," Lloyd explained. "We could hardly begin with such a difficulty after all dis time it's taken even to get started building the railway."

"I suppose not," she agreed.

So at last Lloyd was actively employed, though even then the actual construction did not begin until another several months had passed, for the surveying was complicated in view of the nature of the unpredictable terrain and climate. They were hampered by the rains, by flooding, to say nothing of the difficulty in procuring the gang of navvies from the native population and sorting out who would work where and with whom, in view of all the differing religious beliefs and the strange caste system.

During all this time Captain Richmond was a frequent visitor to the house in Garden Reach where the Fosters continued to stay, though there were periods when he was absent on military matters up-country.

"Won't your friend mind us staying here all this time? Where is he?" Carrie asked him.

The Captain seemed amused. He coughed and then said. "My

friend has no need of this accommodation at present and is most happy for you to stay in his house as long as you wish."

"Yes – but surely we should be paying him some rent?"

"My dear Mrs Foster, I – my *friend* – would not hear of it."

Carrie glanced at him curiously. Suddenly she began to doubt the very existence of the mysterious 'friend' who owned the property. Wisely, she thought it better not to press the matter further.

At long last, when they had been in India over two years, the actual construction work began and Carrie found she had to leave the comfortable house and follow her husband alongside the track of the slowly growing railway. But now her itinerant life bore no resemblance to that harsh life in England under her father's neglectful care. Whenever possible, Lloyd Foster found accommodation for her in proper houses, the homes of people either directly connected with the railway, or at least interested in its growth. If no house were at hand, the camp they set up was like a small village, for not only were there all the railway-workers, but the entourage which Lloyd Foster had collected for himself and his wife, whom he was determined should be treated as a lady, was vast in itself. Carrie laughed at the difference between her life in a mud hut or shack in England to the one here surrounded by servants. But her laughter was tinged with sadness when she thought of the hard life her mother had led, how she had never known such consideration from her husband.

Carrie's tent was elaborate, being twenty feet high and twenty feet square, divided into sleeping quarters and living quarters. Meals were served by her servants with the same ritual as if they were in a palace, and at night the whole camp was surrounded by fires to keep away the tigers and other beasts which roamed the jungle.

Captain Richmond was a frequent visitor to the camp, as he had been to the house in Calcutta.

"Lloyd is not yet home," Carrie told the Captain one evening, meeting him at the entrance to the tent. She was determined not to ask him inside, for the silent Indian servants had a habit of disappearing if they thought their mistress had a guest.

His face was in shadow, but his voice, mocking and yet at the same time challenging, came softly through the darkness. "Perhaps you would care to take a walk around the camp-site, Mrs Foster?"

Silently, she put her hand reluctantly upon his arm and he led her away from her tent, towards the camp-fires set at intervals.

"Ah, what mystery and danger lurks beyond those flames, my dear Mrs Foster."

"Indeed, sir!" Mockingly she adopted his own turn of phrase. "There is much to be feared from the wild animal, almost as much as from civilised man!"

Captain Richmond's eyes were upon her face illuminated by the flickering firelight. She is the most beautiful, fascinating woman I have ever met, he thought. And her coolness towards me arouses my desire for her all the more. I'd like to crush her in my arms, feel her yield to my will . . .

As they walked through the darkness amidst the jungle, he bent towards her. "You have nothing to fear, my dear Mrs Foster, from any *man*. All men would fall at your feet. Such beauty as yours demands adoration."

"I think you mock me, sir."

"Ah, madam, how can you be so cruel? If you were not a married lady, married to a man I most *earnestly* admire, we would not be walking like two friends, so chaste, so distant."

Carrie's heart beat fearfully. He was hinting at his feelings for her. Yet, instead of being flattered by his words, she felt an icy finger of dread amidst the heat of the jungle. She shivered and Captain Richmond was at once all effusive concern.

"Mrs Foster, are you cold? I forget my duty. Pray let me put my coat about your shoulders."

At once he began to unbutton his scarlet tunic.

"No, no, I am not cold. It is merely the jungle – the cries of the birds and the monkeys. It seems so frightening here in the darkness."

"No – I insist," he said and draped his jacket about her.

"Thank you," she murmured, unable to refuse now. "Please, will you take me back to my tent now, Captain?"

Lloyd Foster was waiting at the tent. At the sight of them he started forward. "Carrie – Carrie, my love. Are you all right? What . . .?"

"My dear Foster," the Captain bounded forward. "She is quite safe. We were merely walking when your wife became a little chilled."

Lloyd glanced from Carrie to the Captain's face and back again. "Oh, I see," he said gruffly, obliged to accept Captain Richmond's explanation, but Carrie could see the anguish in his eyes, the unspoken question.

"I will take my leave of you, Mrs Foster." As she gave him back his coat, the Captain took her hand and raised it again to his lips. "Goodnight – goodnight, Foster." He disappeared into the darkness.

As they prepared for sleep that night, Carrie was aware of the feeling of tension between them. At last Lloyd burst out, "I'm beginning to dislike that fellow, to be sure. I don't like to see you with him. I don't – trust him!" He paused and then laughed wryly. "But then, I suppose I don't trust any man wid you, me darlin', now do I?"

Carrie smiled a little sadly, for though Lloyd's words were spoken half in jest, she knew that there was a world of longing behind them. Suddenly she felt compassion for him. He loved her in his own rough way. He had been so good to her. And even though she found herself in a strange land, he saw to it that she was comfortable and lacked for nothing. She reached out suddenly in an unexpected gesture of tenderness, "You have naught to fear from him, Lloyd, for I dislike him myself – intensely, and have done so since first meeting him."

Lloyd caught at her hand, longing in his eyes. Slowly he pulled her to him and took her in his arms. "You never said."

Carrie, within the circle of his embrace, shrugged. "I thought he was important to you. I thought you needed him to help you meet the right people . . ."

"Ach, Carrie me darlin', I can stand on me own two feet. I want to live in no man's debt. Aye, he's been useful, I'll not deny, but

. . ." his embrace tightened about her. "If he's makin' a nuisance of himself to you . . ."

She put her fingers on his lips. "I'll not let him."

Lloyd laughed softly against her. "Aye, an' I believe that, me lovely."

That night his lovemaking was tender and gentle and for the first time Carrie felt herself respond to him through a growing fondness. He was a good, kind man and deserved her love, she thought sadly as later he lay sleeping beside her.

She closed her eyes against the tears. If only I could love him, but there's no room in my heart for anyone but Jamie!

The following morning, Lloyd explained that he was to be away from the camp for a week. "I must look at the land ahead, do another survey, for these damn rivers have a habit of changing their course. And I need to be findin' a new camp-site ahead." He looked down at her with concern. "Now you'll be all right, me darlin'?"

"Of course," she assured him, but she did not feel as confident as she sounded. Despite the fact that the camp was full of people, without Lloyd Foster's strong presence, Carrie felt very much alone in this foreign land.

Two days after his departure the first Indian was taken sick with cholera. Carrie visited her servant, who was lying in his tent. He was vomiting and crying with the pain in his feet. Constantly he cried out weakly for water and yet when she held a cup to his cracked lips he seemed unable to drink. Within twelve hours he was dead. After that the fever swept through the camp so that soon the roles were reversed and the mistress was moving from tent to tent ministering to her servants and to the men who built the railway. Three died the following day and another two the day after that. Work on the railway must have stopped, she thought, but she could not worry about that. Those who were left, lugged the corpses to the river bank and unceremoniously flung them into the water.

The sight of the victims – their brown skin parched and burning to the touch, their already emaciated bodies becoming like skeletons, the dark eyes filled with suffering – touched Carrie's heart. She felt so helpless, all she could do was to keep sponging them down and offering drinks.

"Missus – we put hot rods on the soles of der feet," one servant told her. "Old Indian custom – very good – drive out pain."

Carrie snorted. "The only effect I can see that having is to cause even more pain!"

The Indian shook his head. "Oh, no, Missus – very good. You wanna try?"

"No," she said sharply, lifting the head of one of her patients and holding a wooden bowl to his cracked lips. "I do not – and don't let me hear of you trying it either."

The Indian shrugged philosophically, "They all gonna die anyways," he muttered and padded away.

Carrie felt no fear of disease herself. Had she not nursed her brothers? She had no time to attend to her own appearance, so that by the end of the week when Lloyd was due to return, her hair was ruffled and streaked with dust, her clothes stained, her face hot and her eyes red-rimmed with fatigue.

She longed for her husband's return, for his strength and help, as four more of her servants fell ill. Soon there would be no one left and she would be alone in the camp, alone amidst the horrors of the wild jungle! She lit the fires at night but there was little fuel left and courageous though she was, Carrie dare not venture into the thicket to seek more.

As she stooped to light the fire, she heard the sound of a horse approaching the camp. She stood up.

"Lloyd, oh, Lloyd, thank goodness!" she cried, greatly relieved at the thought of his return. She ran towards the man on horseback and then stopped suddenly.

It was not her husband who had ridden into the camp, but Captain Richmond.

Disappointment and a twinge of fear caught at her.

"My dear Mrs Foster," Jeremy Richmond leapt from his horse and hurried towards her. "Whatever is the matter . . .?"

"I – thought you were – my husband."

"But – you look greatly fatigued. Are you ill?"

"No. No, I'm not. But there is cholera in the camp. The Indians . . ."

"My dear lady, you must remove yourself at once. This is no place for you. If you should contract the disease . . ." Instinctively, he had moved back a pace from her and she could not help a wry smile touching her lips as she noticed his action. She was not so desirable now, she thought, dishevelled and dusty and a possible carrier of disease.

"I cannot leave until my husband returns. Besides the sick need caring for . . ."

"Your husband would not forgive me if I were to leave you here in such danger," Captain Richmond insisted. "Not only danger of contagion but – if all your servants die – what then? You – alone in the jungle? It is unthinkable!"

"I must admit to being a little afraid . . ." then she added firmly, for she guessed what he was leading up to say, "but I cannot leave. I cannot leave these people to die."

Captain Richmond dismissed the matter with a wave of his hand. "They are dispensable. I can obtain you more servants in Calcutta."

Carrie gasped. "How can you be so heartless? They are human beings. They are suffering agonies with this terrible fever . . ."

"Your husband would have no such scruples, ma'am," the Captain's tone was full of sarcasm. "I must insist you return with me to Calcutta. We will leave a message here for Foster on his return."

"I will *not* come with you, Captain Richmond," Carrie said quietly and added reluctantly. "Though I am grateful to you for your thought for my welfare."

"Oh, Carrie, Carrie," he stepped towards her, his eyes wild. He gripped her shoulders. Carrie grew rigid beneath his touch.

"Captain Richmond – you forget yourself!"

Behind them there was the sound of another horse. They both

turned to see Lloyd Foster riding towards them. Captain Richmond released her at once and hurried forward to meet her husband.

"Foster! How glad I am to see you. I have been trying to make your wife see reason. The camp has been hit by a cholera epidemic in your absence, and Carrie – Mrs Foster," he hurried on swiftly to hide his slip of the tongue, but the look in Lloyd Foster's eyes told Carrie that he had noticed the Captain's use of her Christian name in a familiar manner. "Mrs Foster has been nursing them. I cannot emphasise too strongly the danger to herself in this. You should get her away immediately. Leave all your belongings – everything. I pray you, come quickly back to Calcutta, back to my house – my friend's house." Again in his agitation, he made a slip but now concern filled Lloyd Foster's mind so that only Carrie observed it.

Lloyd was down from his horse in an instant and striding towards her. "Ach, me darlin', what have you been doin' to yourself?"

Her head rose in defiance. "I've been nursing the sick, it's my duty, Lloyd. Our duty. We cannot leave these people to die alone – out here in the jungle."

"If you don't leave – and now," Captain Richmond's voice was insistent, "you will all be dead!"

"I may already have the disease on me," Carrie said calmly. "Do you wish me to be the cause of an epidemic in Calcutta?"

The Captain shrugged, whilst Lloyd murmured, "But I should get you away from here."

"Don't be ridiculous, Lloyd," Carrie snapped, impatient with all the arguing. "Of course I shan't get the disease now. I must have an immunity to it. Good grief, haven't I nursed enough sickness with my own brothers?"

But their problem was solved for them in an unexpected way. That night the Indian servants who had not fallen sick fled the camp, and by the morning Carrie and Lloyd found themselves the only two healthy people in the camp. By evening the sick had died, and so there was now no reason for them to remain in camp.

"Leave everything," Captain Richmond, who had again come to visit them, insisted. "Just come home with me and we will engage more servants and workmen for you in Calcutta. No need to tell them you've had the disease here. They'll come back with you in due course."

"Aye, maybe you're right at that," Lloyd Foster agreed, though there was a reluctance in his eyes.

Back in the comfortable surroundings of the house in Garden Reach, Carrie found herself once more cosseted and waited upon. Neither she nor Lloyd contracted cholera and after a few days Captain Richmond insisted that they should use their enforced holiday to become acquainted with some of the Europeans in Calcutta.

"Many of the wealthy merchants are anxious to meet you, Foster," he told Lloyd. "They look upon your railway as a means of transport which will bring greater profits for them, and they wish to show you their hospitality."

So, thought Carrie, it still went on, even out here in India. Men using one another for their own ends. Even though her feelings towards her husband had mellowed considerably through his goodness to her, she could never forget how he and her own father had used Jamie Trent's grandfather – who was her own grandfather too, she remembered suddenly – a drunken, defenceless, old man – to gain possession of his land for the railway.

"Ah, well, dat's good to be sure, but I should be getting back to me railway . . ."

"Oh, surely not. You've not yet found all the men you need, have you?" He glanced sideways at Carrie. "Besides, your wife deserves a change of scene from the nightmare of that camp!"

Lloyd's eyes rested upon his wife. "Well, you're right there, I'm thinkin'."

So they allowed themselves to be swept once more into the social life of the wealthy Europeans in Calcutta. But Carrie was not taken in by it. All this wealth, she thought, and there's people starving in the streets below, dying of dreadful diseases and living in squalor. She sighed. Life, it seemed, was unequal the world over.

"May I have the pleasure of this dance, Mrs Foster?" Captain Richmond was before her, his eyes challenging, his smile mocking.

They were attending a ball given by one of the European merchants in Lloyd Foster's honour.

"Thank you, Captain." She gave him her hand and forced herself to smile charmingly at him.

They moved into the dance.

"May I be permitted to say how beautiful you are looking tonight," Jeremy Richmond murmured.

"Why, thank you."

Her ball gown was pale pink satin, decorated with tiny bows. The neckline was low and the wide, swinging crinoline emphasised her tiny waist.

As the dance ended, Captain Richmond said, "May I be allowed to escort you home? Your husband has become involved in a lengthy game of cards, I believe."

"Do you not play, Captain Richmond?"

"Occasionally, when it suits me."

When he needed to, more like, Carrie thought wryly, just like Lloyd, he would use his gambling instincts to swell his pockets.

Aloud she said, "Thank you, but Lady Benjamin, who lives next door to your house – to your *friend's* house, I should say – has offered me a place in her carriage. Her husband, too, is involved in the same card game as Lloyd." She was glad to have a ready-made excuse, thankful for the kindness of Lady Benjamin. She saw the Captain's anger spark in his eyes, saw his mouth tighten. He took her hand in his and bowed low over it.

"Some other time, ma'am." His words seemed like a veiled threat.

Lloyd did not return that night and when there was still no sign of him the next morning, Carrie became alarmed.

She sent word to Lady Benjamin to see if her husband had returned and was informed that Sir Hugh had come home at about two in the morning.

Where, then, was Lloyd?

The servant, whom she had sent on the errand, bowed low once more. "Lady say to tell you, Missus, that Master go with Captain. Where, she don't know, but he go."

"With Captain Richmond?"

"Ya, Missus."

"Very well, thank you." Now she was even more anxious.

About mid-morning she heard hoofbeats and ran to the window at once. Captain Richmond was dismounting in front of the house, but he was alone.

Carrie bit her lip as she waited for the Captain to be shown into the room.

"Ah, my dear Mrs Foster."

"Where's Lloyd?" she asked without preamble.

"Your husband, ma'am?" The insolence was more apparent now. "I should not have thought you would be particularly worried about your *husband*!"

Carrie gasped. He moved closer, so close she could feel his rapid breath upon her face. "What do you mean, and how dare you speak to me in that – that manner?"

"Oh, I dare, Mrs Foster, because I found out a few things about the beautiful, aloof Mrs Foster last night."

He grasped hold of her shoulders. "Your dear husband was drunk and he started rambling, talking about his life – his married life with you. Oh, he loves you, that's not in doubt. What is in doubt, Mrs Foster," his words were lined with sarcasm. "Is *your* feeling for *him*. From his sometimes incoherent mumblings I managed to piece the truth together. At least, I think it's the truth. That's why I'm here, Carrie my darling, to find out about you, and your so-called marriage."

"Let go of me this instant, or – or I'll scream!"

"Much good it would do you. *My* servants would not come to your rescue."

"So it *is* your house?"

"Of course. I could scarcely tell you that, though, could I, or you would have refused to accept my hospitality?"

"Yes, I would."

"See how well I know you already, my dearest."

Carrie began to struggle but the years of refined living had robbed her of some of her strength. Under Lloyd's protection she had had no need to fight for survival.

Not until now.

"Where is Lloyd?"

"Mr Foster is on his way back to the railway site. I packed him into a gharry and bade three of my servants drive him back."

"He went – without telling me?"

The Captain laughed maliciously. "He had no choice, ma'am. He was dead drunk. By the time he is sober he should be back with his beloved railway."

"There are no navvies there since the cholera."

"Oh, that was taken care of days ago – a party were sent out and should be well settled into camp by now. All that was missing was their master. So I thought that should be rectified."

Carrie grew more angry and a prickle of fear ran down her spine. "Then I, too, must return to the camp."

"Ah now, I have other plans for you, my dear."

"You presume, sir. Whatever your plans are they shall not include me!"

His grip, from which she had been unable to wriggle free, tightened so that his fingers dug into her flesh. "You have kept me at arm's length, so cool and remote, playing the lady. And I thought it was because you loved your husband. But you don't, do you, Mrs Foster? 'If only she loved me', he said last night. 'Why couldn't she love me instead of that Trent fellow?' "

"Oh!" Carrie cried and began to struggle violently. But the more she wriggled, the tighter he held her.

"Ah, now that seems to have struck a chord, doesn't it, my dear Mrs Foster?"

"You are insufferable. Let – me – go!"

"Who is this Trent? Is he your lover?"

"It's – none of your damn business."

"Aha!" His eyes glinted with satisfaction. "So the ladylike mask begins to slip a little, eh?"

"I've never pretended to be a *lady*, as you put it. But Lloyd has money and he wanted to buy me clothes, and . . ."

Jeremy Richmond was laughing. "Lloyd Foster has money? You're living in a fool's paradise, my dear. He owes me five hundred, and

God knows how much more to others interested in his damn railway."

Carrie was suddenly still, horror-stricken by the Captain's words, for she knew he was not lying.

"But – but you're not interested in his railway, are you?"

"No," and his voice grew hoarse with suppressed emotion. "But I am interested in his *wife*!"

Carrie, her face only inches from his, said, "Well, Captain, now your cards are finally on the table, let me tell you this. Husband or no husband, I would never – ever – be interested in you. Now, will you kindly release me or I shall create the biggest commotion ever heard in Calcutta."

For a moment they stood locked in a battle of wills, then with a short laugh he let her go. "I can wait, my love. Now I know the truth about you – and your marriage – I can bide my time. But," he added, and there was menace in his tone. "You shall not escape me. I shall follow you wherever you go – to the ends of the earth if necessary. You shall not escape me – not now!"

He turned and was gone from the room. Carrie sat down, suddenly finding that she was shaking from head to foot. The revelation of her husband's financial state, the Captain's abhorrent advances and his threats, had badly frightened even Carrie's stout heart.

"Lloyd," she said aloud to the empty room. "I must go to Lloyd. I must tell him. He will protect me."

She managed to hire a gharry – a box-like vehicle without springs drawn by a scrawny horse – and soon Calcutta was behind her. As Fort William grew fainter in the distance, Carrie breathed more freely. They travelled for a distance of some thirty miles, passing all the places she had stayed alongside the railway as slowly it had stretched across the countryside during the last eighteen months. The horse was exhausted, but the railway bed was in sight.

As they drew closer, it seemed to Carrie that there was a great deal of shouting and yelling going on. Indian workers were running in all directions, their arms waving, their voices raised in a high-pitched babble. She narrowed her eyes against the glare of the sun. The work in progress was a cutting through a low hill and the railway track had already been laid so far into the cutting, but it stopped dead, hidden by what looked like a landslide.

She jumped down from the vehicle and, picking up her crinoline skirt, she began to run towards the workings. She grabbed an Indian running in the opposite direction. "What has happened?" she demanded, but she had learnt so little of the language that she could understand nothing of his incoherent jabber.

She hurried on, down the embankment, slipping and sliding in her anxiety. She could see Mr Thompson, the new engineer, near the fall, directing the workers, his voice loud and clear, his arms waving directions.

"Mr Thompson, Mr Thompson, what has happened? I'm Mrs Foster – Lloyd's wife."

He turned. His clothes and face were covered with dust, his face streaked as rivulets of sweat ran down his cheeks. Wearily he passed his hand over his forehead.

"Lloyd, where is Lloyd?" Her voice was shrill with fear. She saw him glance towards the pile of rubble, and her heart contracted. "Oh, no!" she whispered.

"There's six under there, ma'am. And I'm pretty sure one's your husband. We're getting to them as fast as we can but . . ." His voice died away, then more briskly, he added, "If you'll excuse me, ma'am. I must help."

"Of course," she said and stood watching, feeling lost and helpless as the men dug and scrabbled at the fall.

How long could anyone live under that, she thought, supposing they even survived the first fall? It was sand and stone mostly. They'd suffocate. It would fill their mouths, their nostrils, their eyes . . .

She gave a small cry of anguish and clasped her arms about her body in a gesture of self-comfort.

After half an hour they retrieved the first body, then swiftly three more were found – all dead.

One of the party of rescuers gave a cry as another body came into view and Carrie's head jerked up. She saw them pull Lloyd's huge frame from beneath the sand and she stumbled forward.

"He's still breathing, Mrs Foster," Mr Thompson said, "but only just!"

They carried him a short distance from the fall and laid him down gently. At once Lloyd began to struggle to rise.

"No, no, lie back," Carrie insisted, kneeling beside him and cradling his head in her lap. He began to cough and splutter, gasping and wheezing. She brushed the sand and dirt away from his face.

"Carrie, Carrie, is that you?" his voice was a strangled whisper.

"Yes, now lie still. We'll get help."

"No, no time," he whispered desperately. "I can't breathe – I can't breathe." He began to choke.

He drew rasping breath then said, "Carrie, you must get home. Go straight home to England. Don't stay – here. He's dangerous. Get away!" She knew he meant Captain Richmond. "Do you hear me – now?"

"Lloyd, don't talk . . ."

"I must – tell you. Go back to – to – Trent." As if he had only lived to see her once more, to speak to her again, to tell her what she must do, he fell back, his eyes staring blankly towards the sky.

"Lloyd! *Lloyd*!" she cried and shook him.

" 'Tis no use, ma'am. He's gone. The stuff must have choked his lungs. I don't know how he lasted that long in there," Mr Thompson said in wonderment.

Slowly Carrie lifted her face. She said nothing but silently she thought – you don't know the strength of this man. And now his strength was gone. His protection was gone. She was alone in a strange, hostile country at the mercy of Jeremy Richmond.

The dead were buried with little ceremony at the side of the railway. As Carrie stood above the grave marked by a simple, rough cross made out of railway builder's tools, she felt real grief for her husband. If only I could have loved him, she thought with remorse. Although she could not forgive many of the things he had done, she had to admit that his treatment of her had always been loving and thoughtful. Knowing she loved another man, he had married her, lavished gifts on her, protected her and tried to make her a lady. Her life with him had been one of comfort and luxury such as she had never before known. As she turned away she knew that, though her love would always belong to Jamie Trent and to no other, Lloyd Foster had earned her tender affection.

Chapter Seven

Carrie stepped down from the train at Abbeyford Halt. The train pulled away from her, thundering up the line, past Abbeyford Manor and out of the valley. She looked about her in wonder. How altered everything was. The railway line ran exactly where her father and Lloyd Foster had planned it, between the Manor and the stream, the common and farmland cut in two by the embankment supporting the track.

The Manor! Her heart missed a beat. Was he there? Was Jamie Trent still living there?

She walked along the small wooden platform, through the white-painted gate that marked the boundary of the railway property and began to walk towards the village. Now the cottages were stained black with the constant smoke from the steam engines. She neared the line of cottages where her grandmother, Sarah Smithson lived. A little nervously, she approached the door, but as she lifted her hand to knock she felt a sense of desolation sweep over her and knew there was no longer anyone living in this cottage, even before she wiped away the grime from the window and peered in. Then she tried the door and found it opened, scraping on the stone floor. She stepped into the dismal, damp cottage. The place was derelict. Odd items of furniture still littered the dirty floor, a broken chair, broken cups, old clothes and dust – dust everywhere. The cottage had been empty for some time.

Carrie felt the sadness sweep over her. Her grandmother was dead – she sensed it, knew it. And probably Henry Smithson too. There was nothing for her here. She left the cottage reluctantly, closing the door behind her as if closing the door on her memories of the little old woman who had lived there. She wished she had known her better, wished she could have known the truth of her grandmother's love affair with Guy Trent.

Carrie looked up and down the village street and then her gaze was pulled once more across the village green and up, up towards Abbeyford Manor. Her heart began to beat a little faster. She had to know whether or not Jamie still lived there – if he was marriediwith a family of his own – or If he still remembered her.

She walked up the lane, over the tiny bridge near the ford and then over the new railway bridge – a slim young woman in a wine-coloured skirt and jacket of fine velvet material, edged with self-coloured braid. Her black hair was smooth and neat, coiled up on the top of her head, upon which perched a pretty bonnet.

It was autumn of 1853 and the golden leaves were falling from the hedgerows, and the air was clear and sharp.

Carrie breathed in the country air, savouring its freshness which even the presence of the railway and all its smoke could not spoil completely. It was so invigorating after the heat and humidity of India. It was so quiet, so peaceful – almost too quiet. She glanced back thoughtfully towards the village. There were one or two people moving about, but many of the cottages seemed deserted now. Perhaps, with the ruination of the farming land by the railway, many families had been forced to move elsewhere to find work.

So much had happened during the years she had been away, so much had changed and yet now she was back here again, the years between seemed to have gone so quickly.

Would Jamie have changed? Would he look the same? Would he *feel* the same about her?

"Go home," had been Lloyd's dying words to her. "Get away from here – go back to Trent!"

She had been lucky to escape from India in the way that she had done. After Lloyd had been buried she had returned briefly to Captain Richmond's house. Luckily, he was not there. She learnt he had been sent at short notice with a detachment of soldiers up-country. Silently thanking Providence, she had swiftly packed as much as she could carry. Taking her jewel box she had found her way to the markets in the streets of Calcutta and, after much haggling, had sold her jewels for enough money to buy her a passage home. Her only fear was that there would be no ship in Calcutta harbour bound for England. But once again she was fortunate. Threading her way through the busy dockside, she had heard the English voice of a First Mate shouting at his idle crew as they loaded cargo on to the ship.

Minutes later when she faced the Captain of the ship and requested passage, she knew a moment's fear as he said gruffly, "This ain't no passenger ship, lady. You'd best be waitin' till next week . . ."

"Captain, I cannot wait till next week. I must leave India at once. My husband has been killed in a railway building accident, and I . . ."

"Building the railway, was he?" Interest had sparked in the man's eyes. "Ah, well now, there's a man after me own heart. Me brother's a Hingineer on a railway back home in England. Now, I'd be right glad to help you, ma'am, but the cabin'll be a bit rough. An' I can only take you to France, ma'am."

"I don't mind one bit, Captain," Carrie had smiled and silently had blessed the Captain's 'hingineer' brother. "I can find something else from there, I'm sure."

The passage home had taken over three months. Three months in which she had been able to rest and recover her composure after Lloyd's death and her hurried departure from Captain Jeremy Richmond's clutches.

Now finally – after several more weeks – she was back in Abbeyford and the years between seemed to slip away.

As she stood at the gate leading into the stableyard of the Manor, Carrie hesitated, irresolute. If he were still here, how could she just burst in upon him? What if he had a wife and children? Would it not be wrong of her to disturb the peace he had perhaps found for himself? And yet, her own heart ached for sight of him. She knew, deep down, that whatever his situation now, his love for her had been so deep that even the passage of these last twelve years could not have dimmed that love.

She walked through the deserted yard, everywhere was neglected and overgrown. The stables were tumble-down, the weeds growing through the cobbled yard. Jamie cannot live here now, she thought with sudden disappointment. He would never allow it to become like this – unless, unless he had lost all heart, all ambition with her going.

She knocked on the back door, but there was no reply so she walked round to the front of the house and pulled on the stiff bell-rope there. She waited for what seemed a long time until she heard shuffling footsteps approach the door.

It opened slowly and Carrie found herself staring at a stranger – a woman of about her own age. She wore a low-cut silk dress which once must have been a fine ball gown, but now it was rumpled and stained. Her hair was piled up untidily on to her head, tendrils hanging down around her face.

"What d'you want?" Her voice was rough and her manner coarse.

Carrie's mouth felt suddenly dry. "Does – Mr Trent live here?"

There was a moment's silence as the woman eyed Carrie. "And if he does, what do you want wi' him?"

Carrie almost gasped in astonishment. Surely, surely not *Jamie*? She squared her shoulders meeting the woman's hostile eyes calmly. "I'd like a word with him, if you please?"

"Oh, 'I'd like a word with him, if you please'," the woman mimicked mockingly. "What'd he want wi' the likes o' you?"

I might well ask the same question of you, Carrie thought but aloud she repeated, "I would like to see him, please," with far more confidence in her tone than she felt.

Oh Jamie, Jamie, her heart cried out. Not this!

"You'd best come in then," the woman turned, leaving the door open for Carrie to enter and follow. She flung open the door of what had once been Squire Guy Trent's study and stood aside for Carrie to enter the room.

"There he is – but I doubt you'll get much sense out of him jus' now. Been drunk for two days, 'ee has."

The smell of drink hit her forcibly as Carrie stepped into the small room. She blinked and as her eyes became accustomed to the dimness of the room, she saw the figure of a man sprawled across the desk, an empty whisky bottle on its side. His head was resting on one arm, a few inches from his limp hand. She almost spoke the name aloud – Squire Trent – for this is how she had last seen him. Then she checked herself. No, no, he was dead, by his own hand. Jamie had told her. Then who ...?

She walked round the desk until she could see his face and when she did she drew breath sharply in surprise. "Pa!"

It was indeed her father. At the sound of her voice Evan stirred and raised bleary, bloodshot eyes to squint up at her. Carrie's heart missed a beat. It was as if she were seeing a ghost, for now her father was the image of the defenceless, pathetic old man she remembered as Squire Guy Trent – Evan's own father!

"Oh, Pa, what are you doing here?"

The woman, who had stood in the doorway watching, now moved into the room. "Is 'ee your Pa, then? Well, I niver!"

Carrie looked up at the woman. "Calls himself Trent, does he?"

The woman looked surprised. "Yea. Why, ain't that 'is name, then?"

Carrie smiled sadly. "It used to be 'Smithson'."

The sound of her voice, or the use of his former name, roused Evan. "Me name's Trent. I've a right to the name of Trent – it's my birthright!"

Carrie leaned closer. "Pa, it's Carrie."

The blurred eyes squinted at her. "Carrie? Ha – told you I'd live here one day, didn't I?"

"Much good it seems to have done you," she said candidly.

"I got a right to be here." He banged the desk with his clenched fist and swept the empty bottle to the floor. The sound of shattering glass made the two women jump.

"You 'is daughter, then?" the woman asked Carrie. "Well I never knew 'ee was even married!"

"Where is my mother?" Carrie asked.

"Lord knows," the woman shrugged. "Taken me in proper, 'ee 'as." Her glance rested balefully on the sprawling form.

"Does anyone else live here?"

"No, only us two."

"Pa," she shook his shoulder. "Pa – where's Ma and the boys?"

"Gone, all gone."

"Where – where've they gone?"

"Dead – all dead," he moaned and slumped forward again.

Carrie caught her breath and she and the woman gazed at each other.

"Ee, love, I'm right sorry to hear that." For the first time there was friendliness in the woman's tone. "You bin away then? Didn't you know?"

Carrie shook her head. "I've been away for almost twelve years." She paused then asked. "Do you know who lived here before Mr – Trent?" Referring to her father by that name did not come easily, but it was the only name by which this woman knew him.

"No," she shook her head. " 'Ee was here when I came. I met him in Manchester, an' he brought me back 'ere."

Carrie sighed and looked down with sadness at her father. He'd achieved his bitter ambition – to ruin the Trents and to live in the Manor House himself. But it had not brought him any happiness. In so doing he had ruined himself also.

"There's nothing for me here," she turned away and walked slowly from the room, past the woman and out of the house.

"Come an' see 'im again – when he's sober," the woman called after her, but Carrie only smiled faintly and nodded. She passed through the silent stableyard, averting her eyes from the buildings – that was where poor Guy Trent had ended his useless, tragic life. Once in the lane she turned to the left and climbed towards the wooded brow of the hill. Sadly she wandered through the shadows, hardly knowing where her footsteps led her. So many memories came crowding back. Memories of those wonderful days of summer. Memories of the handsome young man she had loved and still loved to this day.

She paused at the edge of the wood to look at the abbey ruins and then was drawn towards them.

The ruins had changed little. The ground within the crumbling walls was still littered with rubble, and the little room was still intact. If she had been more of a fanciful nature she might have imagined she heard the echoing laughter of the happy, ghostly lovers. Herself and Jamie? Or Guy Trent and his Sarah?

She shuddered and turned away down the hill towards the village. The bright day seemed to mock her sadness. She was no nearer, now, of finding Jamie again than she had been when she had left India. If anything she was even farther away, for then she had pictured him still living here.

Fondly – romantically – she had imagined him still living in Abbeyford Manor. Her heart had woven the fantasy of a joyful, poignant reunion. Her arrival at the Manor, Jamie's strong arms about her, the haven of love she sought.

But he was no longer here.

He had gone, and all that was left was her drunken, pathetic father, now the image of the man – his own father – whom he had hated with such venom all his life; on whom he had sought – and achieved – such a terrible revenge!

But his revenge had destroyed them all.

Where was Jamie now? Where could he have gone? Who would know?

Her steps led her automatically to the churchyard set in the centre of the village. She pushed open the gate and went in. Walking among the gravestones, without thinking she began to search for those of her mother and brothers.

"May I help you?" A kindly voice spoke behind her making her jump.

She turned round to see the smiling face of a young curate. "Oh – I – er – don't quite know."

"Were you looking for a particular grave?" he asked gently.

She nodded. "I've been away for almost twelve years. I have only just learnt that my mother and younger brothers are – dead. I wondered . . ."

"Perhaps I can help. I could look in the Parish Register, if you like."

Carrie nodded. "That would be very kind of you. I'd like to know – where they are."

"Come along, then," the young man said briskly and led the way into the quiet dimness of the church and through into the vestry.

He pulled a huge book from a shelf and laid it on the table. "Now, can you give me some details."

"Well, there's Lucy Smithson and her two sons, Matthew and Thomas."

"And you've been left about twelve years?"

"Yes."

His finger was running down the pages.

"Smithson . . ." he murmured. "Ah now, here's a *Luke* Smithson."

Sadness swept over Carrie at the memory of her elder brother. "Yes – yes, he died just before I left."

"Ah – so the names you are looking for would be later than that." There was a short pause when he said. "Now here we are – Matthew and Thomas Smithson. Oh dear me, their deaths are listed on the same date. Now, wait a minute, I seem to remember. Yes, were they working on the building of the railway?"

Carrie nodded.

"Yes, *now* I remember. There was an explosion – dynamite incorrectly placed, I believe. There were seven killed, I think." He counted the names in the register. "Yes, seven. And I'm afraid your brothers were amongst that number."

"And my mother – Lucy Smithson."

Again he searched. "Yes – here it is. She died only two months after your brothers."

Carrie nodded again, a lump in her throat. She could imagine poor, worn-out Lucy, finally beaten by the loss of her two youngest children. Of all of the seven children Lucy had borne, only Carrie now survived.

"Could you also look for a Sarah Smithson? She was my grandmother."

For several moments his finger ran on down the page. Slowly he shook his head. "No – I can't see any Sarah. There's a *Henry* Smithson. He died eight years ago."

"Yes. He was – her husband." Carrie hesitated for he had not been her grandfather. That was Squire Trent.

Suddenly, a thought struck Carrie. "Wait a minute. Go back a little. To the time when Squire Guy Trent died."

The young curate made no comment, but did as she asked.

"Why, yes, her name is directly after his. She died the following week." His eyes were upon Carrie, questioningly, but even though the young man had been so kind she did not want to confide in him.

Let the unhappy lovers' secret die with them, and she thought how ironic it was that they had been obliged to live out their lives apart and yet in death their names were close beside each other.

"Can you tell me where my mother and brothers are buried, please?"

"Ah, yes, now where are we?" He looked back at the list again, noted the numbers of the graves and then from the back of the book pulled out a plan of the graves in the churchyard. "Yes, they're all together over by the yew tree in the far corner." Again he turned, almost apologetically, towards her. "Their graves are unmarked, I'm afraid. No one requested any head stones and the parish cannot . . ."

"No, no, of course not," Carrie said swiftly. Her father would never have thought to spend his money on such things as gravestones! Sooner a bottle of whisky, she thought bitterly.

It was quiet and peaceful under the yew tree in the corner of the churchyard. Probably the only peace her mother had ever known, Carrie thought sadly, and wished she could have done more to make her mother's life easier. The grass was long and the area neglected, but she could just detect the gentle mounds showing where her mother and brothers were buried. At last she turned away, sick at heart that, at the moment, she could not afford to erect headstones either. "Some day, some day . . ." she promised the silent earth.

Then intruding into her quiet solitude came the sound of a train whistle as it neared Abbeyford Halt, then moments later it burst into view, puthering clouds of grey smoke. Fascinated, and yet partially appalled by the iron monster thundering through the quiet valley, Carrie watched it screech to a brief stop at the Halt and then, with much chugging, it pulled away and was soon gone, leaving only the tell-tale cloud of smoke drifting over the village.

It was beginning to grow dusk, she had allowed that train to depart without her, and she doubted that there would be another that day. Besides, she was not yet ready to leave Abbeyford. Surely there must be someone here who knew where Jamie had gone. But who?

"Of course," she murmured aloud and a small smile of fresh hope curved her mouth. "His stepmother – Lady Adelina Lynwood!"

She remembered Jamie's words all those years before – could almost hear his beloved voice; 'She's very beautiful and has been very kind to me. I'm very fond of her.'

Jamie would not leave without telling his stepmother where he was going. She would go and see Lady Lynwood, and with that thought her feet began to move eagerly up the lane, then she stopped. It was too late now to walk the several miles from Abbeyford to Lynwood Hall. She could hardly arrive there late at night.

Carrie decided she would stay here in Abbeyford and visit Lady Lynwood the next day. But where could she stay? She could not – would not – go back to the Manor. She wandered down the one village street and found herself outside the cottage which had been her grandmother's. It was empty and cold; she thought, but it offered shelter. There could be no harm in her staying there overnight.

The cottage was lonely, haunted with memories of the old couple who had lived there.

Carrie found a few bits of wood in the coal-house at the back and built a fire in the living-room grate. Though the chimney smoked a little through lack of use, the fire warmed her. She drew the old rickety armchair towards the blaze and banged the cushions vigorously to get rid of the dust, then she curled up in it and despite the fact that it was now several hours since she had eaten, she soon fell asleep.

The morning found her cramped and even more hungry and cold, for the fire had burnt down whilst she had slept.

She splashed her face and hands under the creaking pump in the small backyard and tidied her hair. Then, since there was nothing she could breakfast on, she left the cottage and began the long walk over the hills to Lynwood Hall.

At the Hall, the butler led her into the morning room. Carrie dropped a curtsy and said, "It is kind of you to see me, your ladyship."

"Please be seated," Lady Adelina indicated the wide window-seat near her, where she was sitting, some embroidery in her lap.

"Thank you," Carrie said and moved across the room and sat down. Now that she was closer she could see that Lady Adelina had scarcely altered since the last time she had seen her – over twelve years previously. Her rich auburn hair was just as beautiful with not a trace of grey and her lovely face showed not the faintest line or blemish. She was staring at Carrie, a slightly puzzled expression in her eyes. "Should I know you, Mrs Foster?" she murmured. "I can't seem to recall . . ."

"My lady – we did meet once, but the circumstances, *my* circumstances, were very different then." She trembled a little inwardly, but met Lady Lynwood's gaze with an outward show of fearlessness. "I am Evan Smithson's daughter."

Hatred and fear swept across Lady Adelina's face, then she touched her forehead with trembling fingers and tried to smile. "I'm sorry, my dear, it was just a shock to hear his name again . . ."

Carrie leaned forward, no longer afraid. Lady Lynwood did not resent her, though she obviously felt a deep, abiding hatred for Evan Smithson.

"Why do you hate him so much?"

Lady Lynwood met her clear, questioning gaze. "My dear, it would be very wrong of me to tell you. Just let me say that something he – he did, caused me a great deal of unhappiness. I cannot forgive him – though I know I should."

"It seems," Carrie said quietly, "his bitterness and twisted soul has touched many lives – and – brought unhappiness to them all."

"I'm afraid so."

"You know he is living in Abbeyford Manor now and calling himself Trent?"

Lady Lynwood gasped. "No! No, I didn't. We have severed all connections with Abbeyford now – even though it is only a few miles away. We sold Abbeyford Grange – my grandfather's old home – so there is no need for me to visit Abbeyford now. I went there once, just after the railway line was completed, but to me the village has been spoilt."

Carrie nodded, then said, "Lady Lynwood, the reason for my visit is – to ask you – if – if you know," the colour rose in her cheeks and her heart beat faster, "where Jamie Trent is?"

"Jamie?" Lady Lynwood gazed at her for a moment then she smiled. "Of course, he told me. You and he fell in love, but your father and – another man, I forget his name . . ."

"Lloyd Foster," Carrie interposed. "They came between us, and I was tricked into marrying Lloyd."

"And now?" Lady Adelina asked.

Carrie's shoulders slumped. "I suppose it's too late. I expect Jamie's married, with a family."

"What of your husband?" Lady Adelina probed gently.

"He was killed – in India. I have only just returned to England myself. I came straight here – to Abbeyford – but my father, he's too drunk for me to make any sense of him."

Lady Lynwood's mouth hardened. "He doesn't seem to have found much happiness himself either."

Carrie shook her head. "But Jamie? Do you know where he is, how he is?"

Slowly Lady Lynwood shook her head sadly. "My dear, I wish I *could* help you. Shortly after you left, he came to stay here at Lynwood Hall for a while. Then he decided he would go right away – so he joined the British Army. I hear from him very occasionally, but it is over two years since I last had a brief letter, so I really don't know where he could be now."

Carrie felt the tears prick her eyelids. Her disappointment was acute. She had been so hopeful that Lady Lynwood would know where he was.

"I'm sure he's never married, my dear," Lady Adelina leaned forward and gently touched Carrie's hand. "He would have written to tell me *that*, I know."

Carrie nodded but she was not convinced. Two years since Lady Adelina had last had word from him. So much could have happened in that time . . .

Carrie stood up. "You have been most kind, my lady. Thank you for receiving me."

"I'm so sorry I cannot be of more help. Where will you go now?"

Carrie shrugged, desolate and lost. "I don't know."

"May I suggest London," Lady Adelina said gently. "I believe there are many headquarters and officers' clubs and so on there. You may be able to get news of him. And if," she added, "you need help, we have a town house in Mayfair."

"No – no, I wouldn't presume. You have been so kind already."

"Well, send me word of your address and if I hear anything from him, I promise I will write and let you know."

"You are very good, my lady," Carrie said gratefully.

Lady Adelina smiled. "He mentioned you only once while he was here. He was very unhappy at losing you, I could see that. I'll do whatever I can to help you find each other again."

With Lady Lynwood's promise to cling to, Carrie left Lynwood Hall and returned to Abbeyford. She would catch the next train to London – the very next train! There was now no reason for her to stay in Abbeyford any longer.

Passing the Manor, she hesitated. Perhaps she should just see her father once more before she left. Have one more try. Perhaps by some chance he knew more than Lady Lynwood, though she knew it was unlikely.

"Oh, hello," the woman greeted her in a friendly manner. She was still wearing the same dress she had worn the previous day. "He's sobered up a bit this morning. But he don't remember you comin' yesterday." She held open the door for Carrie to pass into the dismal hall. "I've been tellin' him, but I don't reckon he believes me. Evan," she raised her voice shrilly. "Evan, she's 'ere again. Your girl. Come on," the woman beckoned her through into a room which had once been the drawing-room. It was large and could have been beautiful, but the furniture was dusty, the paintwork peeling and the carpet worn into holes.

Evan Smithson was sprawling on the sofa in front of a blazing fire. His head turned jerkily, and it seemed to take a few moments for his eyes to focus upon her. He still had the manner of a man in a permanent state of drunkenness, though Carrie could see that today he was a little more aware of his surroundings.

"My God! Is it really you, lass?"

Carrie stood before him. "It is, Pa."

"Where've you come from? Where's – what's 'is name?"

"Can't you even remember the name of the man you forced me to marry?" Carrie asked bitterly. "He's dead. He was building a railway in India and he was killed in a landslide."

"So you've come back home, have you? Well, we'll have to clear a room out . . ." he made as if to straggle up.

"There's no need, Pa. I'm not staying. I've only come to ask one thing of you. Do you know where Jamie Trent is now?"

Her father slumped back against the sofa. His mouth trembled and his eyes darted from side to side. His shaking fingers plucked at the worn material of the sofa. "Trent? Trent? Tha's my name."

"No, it isn't, Pa. Your name is *Smithson*!"

"No, no," he shouted, breathing heavily.

" 'Ere, watch it," the woman spoke up. "Don't upset him. He's had one heart attack. I don't want him havin' another."

"That's *my* name," he mumbled. "Squire Guy Trent was my father. It's my birthright."

"I know, Pa. I know," Carrie said soothingly, with far more patience than she felt. "But do you know where his grandson, Jamie Trent, is now?"

"Grandson? Grandson? I don't remember no grandson. His son, Wallis – but he's dead, isn't he?" He grinned suddenly, showing

114

blackened, broken teeth. "Killed trying to save his horse from a fire I started."

"You seem proud of the fact," Carrie said with disgust. Her father grunted.

It was no use, she thought. He couldn't even remember Jamie – or wouldn't! She turned to leave, then briefly looked back over her shoulder. "Pa – why does Lady Adelina Lynwood hate you?"

"Adelina? Ah, my lovely Adelina, my proud beauty!" He laughed cruelly. "Robbed her of her maidenhead, didn't I? Thought she was better than me. I showed her. Wallis Trent wasn't going to have her before me."

Carrie turned away feeling physically sick. His whole life had been spent in bitter resentment of his unfortunate birth. Instead of rising above his illegitimacy, he had allowed it to warp his mind and soul and had destroyed everything and everyone he had touched. Even himself.

Carrie left the Manor and went towards the tiny railway platform to wait for the next train to London.

She would never see her father again, for she guessed that, in that pitiful state, he could not survive for many more months.

Chapter Eight

London was a vast and lonely place and the small amount of money she had had left after paying for her passage home would not last very much longer. Her heart wanted only to search for Jamie, but common sense told her she must find shelter and employment first. But what could she do? Her only experience had been of housework – and the keeping of the shack was scarcely the same as working in a fine house as a maid. She found cheap lodgings and then began searching for work. Carrie applied for one or two positions as housemaid but was turned away. She was even unsuitable for the post of kitchen-maid it seemed.

Winter came, but Carrie had no money to buy warmer clothes – clothes such as she had not needed in the heat of India. New Year arrived, but except for the odd temporary job, lasting only a few days at a time, Carrie still had not found permanent employment. And still she had no news of Jamie, in spite of numerous enquiries.

Then suddenly the cold weather was gone and a warm spring arrived. At least now she was no longer shivering.

One evening when she returned to her dismal lodgings, she found the house in a turmoil. The landlady, a fat, loudmouthed individual, was standing at the top of the stairs banging on the door of a room opposite to the one Carrie occupied.

"You bring that woman out o' there, Mister. I'll have no sickness here in my house." Again she banged on the door.

"What is it, Mrs Prince? What's the matter?" Carrie asked.

"Cholera! That's what," she panted, wheezing, heavily. "I don't want no sickness in my house." She shook her fist towards Carrie as if she were personally responsible.

Carrie stood still on the stairs as the memories of the camp in India swept over her, the natives dying of the dreadful disease.

"Mrs Prince – let me try. I was among cholera in India. I'm not afraid."

"I want 'er out of here. There's a place run by a Miss Nightingale – a cholera house – in Harley Street. She can go there."

"Perhaps you'd call a cab then, while I try to talk to the husband."

"A cab? An' who's to pay for that, might I ask?"

Carrie raised her eyebrows. "Which do you prefer? The price of a cab against her staying here in your house?"

Grumbling, the woman turned and waddled downstairs.

Carrie knocked on the door. "Mr Smith – please open the door. It's Mrs Foster from across the landing." There was no response. "Mr Smith – I know something about cholera. I've been amongst it. I want to help you. Please – open the door."

Nothing happened for a few moments, then Carrie heard the key turn in the lock and the door opened a fraction. Two frightened brown eyes peered round the door.

"Has she gone – Mrs Prince?" He was thin and undernourished himself, dressed only in trousers and a dirty striped shirt and waistcoat. He still wore his cap even in the house.

"Yes, let me come in. I want to talk to you."

Once inside the cramped, airless room, Carrie quickly saw that the woman lying on the rough bed in the corner was very sick. She was writhing, and moaning and dribbling. The whole room smelt sour with sickness. Swiftly, Carrie explained in whispers to the man that his wife must have some proper care. "Mrs Prince knows of a cholera house. Let your wife go there. It's her only chance!"

"No, no, it's the workhouse she means."

"Nonsense – but we will go with her to make sure Mrs Prince is speaking the truth."

The door of No 1 Harley Street was opened by a maid in a black dress with a frilled white apron and cap. "Yes'm?"

"We have a woman sick with cholera," Carrie said. "We have been told we might bring her here."

"Oh, no, madam. This is an Institution for Sick *Gentlewomen*. We can't take – just anyone!"

Carrie opened her mouth to protest but at that moment a quiet voice spoke behind the maid. "What is it, Mary?"

The maid turned and curtsied. "Begging your pardon, Miss Nightingale, there's someone at the door with a woman sick with cholera. She thinks she can bring her here."

The door opened wider and Carrie looked up to see a tall woman, slim and dignified, dressed completely in black. Her calm face was surrounded by short brown hair and her grey eyes were alert and bright. "I am Miss Nightingale. May I help you?" Her voice was pleasant and her pronunciation beautiful. She was undoubtedly a lady of quality, Carrie thought instantly.

Carrie repeated her story.

"I am so sorry, what my maid tells you is perfectly correct. This establishment is for gentlewomen only, and I couldn't take the risk of a cholera patient here either. Take her to the Middlesex Hospital. She will be well cared for there."

"Thank you. We'll do that." Carrie turned away and hurried back to the anxious little man in the cab.

"What'd she say?"

"They can't take her here. We've to take her to the Middlesex Hospital."

"Oh, no!" the little man groaned. "She won't come out of one of them places!"

Grimly, Carrie was forced to agree.

But little Mrs Smith did recover – though she was one of the very few people who survived the dreadful sickness. Perhaps she owed her recovery in no small measure to the devotion of one particular nurse – Mrs Carrie Foster. As soon as Mrs Smith had been admitted to the hospital, Carrie had applied to become a nurse there and was taken on immediately.

"It looks as if we could be at the beginning of an epidemic," the Matron sighed. "Inexperienced though you are, I can make good use of you. I shall be glad to have someone who is not afraid of infection. It will make a change!" she added wryly.

As the spring of 1854 turned into summer the cholera epidemic which had threatened broke out in earnest. The hospitals were stretched to bursting point. Several nurses fell victim to the disease and others fled, fearing for their lives. Carrie worked long and hard amongst the crowded wards – so crowded that some beds were occupied by two women. Others lay on palliasses – or, as more and more patients flooded in, on the bare floorboards – between the beds and down the centre of the ward. There was little the nurses could do to cure the victims of cholera. They could only try to alleviate their discomfort by washing them, offering drinks, or holding the hand of the dying.

It was here at the Middlesex Hospital that Carrie met Miss Nightingale again, for in August that lady came to help organise the nursing of cholera patients. So hectic were the days, so exhausted was she at the end of them, that Carrie had little time and even less energy to continue her search for Jamie. She had written to several officers' clubs, enquiring if he were a member, she had even written to army officials, asking for information as to his regiment and posting, but all enquiries had proved useless.

Then, as weariness and desolation threatened to break down even Carrie's strength of purpose, a letter arrived from Lady Lynwood.

'I have just learned that Jamie's regiment has been posted to the Crimea. I understand he sailed last week.'

Carrie sat with the letter in her hand, loneliness and misery sweeping over her. He had left England, he had been here, somewhere quite near perhaps, and she had not known, and now he was gone, away across the sea to fight a war they had only just begun to hear of.

The weeks passed and the cholera epidemic abated and the hospital began to return to something like normality.

It was ironic, Carrie thought, that now that she had a little more time, there was nothing she could do. Jamie was in a far-off country and she was a virtual prisoner here in England.

At the beginning of October, Carrie received a terse note from Miss Nightingale.

"Please come to see me tomorrow at No 49 Belgrave Square at 11 a.m."

Carrie was shown into the dining-room of the home of Mr Sydney Herbert, Secretary at War, at two minutes to eleven the following morning. Miss Nightingale was seated at the dining-table, papers spread out before her, her pen poised in the act of writing copious notes. She was plainly dressed, her brown hair, parted in the centre and looped in two plaits over her ears. The grey eyes in the oval face regarded Carrie searchingly.

Without preamble, she launched into the reason for her summons. "I have been asked to take a party of nurses to the Crimea. Will you come?"

Carrie gasped. The Crimea? She was being asked to go to the Crimea? It seemed like a dream. She could find Jamie, or at least, her reason told her, she would stand a better chance of hearing news of him than stuck here in England.

"Oh, yes, yes. I will." She could not stop her eagerness from showing on her face.

"It will be demanding, back-breaking work, it will tax your strength, your resolve and your courage to the utmost. You will see sights you had never thought existed. I know of your work at the Middlesex Hospital – it does you credit. But I know nothing of your experience before that?" The statement was a question.

"I nursed my brothers when they died from consumption. Last year I returned from India – my late husband was a railway builder." She paused as Lloyd's laughing face was in her mind's eye. "There was much sickness in India – particularly cholera. I helped out when necessary."

Carrie was not one to boast of her self-sacrifice and yet Miss Nightingale's shrewd eyes seemed to read on her face that here was a woman who had had experience of life. It was written in her eyes.

"Have you any ties in England? Any family or – attachments?"

Carrie shook her head and answered quickly, perhaps too quickly. "No – there's no one here now."

Miss Nightingale's eyebrows rose fractionally but she asked no more questions on that point. She went on to explain the work which would be required of Carrie, finishing with the words, "I am a strict disciplinarian and any transgression from my rules will be severely dealt with. Do you still want to come?"

"Yes – I do."

Miss Nightingale smiled and her face altered immediately, the stern lines relaxing, but only for a moment for then she added seriously, "I don't know what we're going to find out there, Mrs Foster. I hope you will have the stomach for it."

Carrie smiled, remembering the harshness of her life as it had been before she had married Lloyd Foster. "I think I shall, Miss Nightingale."

"Good," Miss Nightingale said briskly. "We leave on Saturday, the day after tomorrow. Can you be ready?"

Carrie felt a surge of excitement. "Yes, ma'am, I can."

She was on her way to find Jamie!

It was a motley selection of women who finally staggered ashore at the Scutari landing-stage. The *Vectis*, in which the party had travelled, had docked at Constantinople and the last mile of the journey, across the Bosphorus, had been made in two caiques. Carrie, least affected by the *mal de mer* of all the party, helped her companions.

"Gawd luv us," exclaimed one 'nurse', a woman recently released from prison, "w'ot 'ave we let ourselves in fer?"

"What indeed," murmured Carrie. Some of the younger girls sank to the ground, whilst the Sisters, Roman Catholic nuns, accepted the trials in silence, but they were white-faced and, Carrie noticed, their hands were shaking.

Carrie looked about her. The whole shoreline was a vast cemetery.

In the rough ground were row upon row of gravestones of various sizes.

Near the landing-stage were a few Turks and, scarcely recognisable, their uniforms were so torn and dirty, were some British soldiers. All pride was gone, their faces were grey with sickness and suffering. Two walked on crutches, one trouser leg hanging loose and empty. Another nursed an empty sleeve, his eyes staring and vacant. Another ranted and raved, weaving about as if drunk until he slumped down on to the ground. No one went to his aid, no bearers appeared to carry him to the hospital. The man just lay there.

Carrie shuddered. Was her Jamie here – one of these pathetic creatures?

The hospital? Carrie's eyes lifted towards the huge, square building, three storeys high, with a red-tiled roof and a tower at each corner, set high up on top of the hill above the landing-stage and the small village.

They began to climb the muddy, winding track leading to the British Barrack Hospital – their home for the next few months at least!

It was not what they had expected. Nothing ever was, Carrie thought ruefully. The party of nurses, not at all welcomed by the officials, were housed in the north-west tower. The party had been here several days and yet they had scarcely set foot outside their cramped quarters. Miss Nightingale remained adamant that she would do nothing until asked to do so by the Senior Medical Officer of the Hospital, a Dr Menzies.

"But men are dying whilst we sit here," Carrie had dared to argue. "Why can't we begin the work we came here to do?"

Miss Nightingale's face had softened. "My dear, your sentiments are admirable, but I fear misplaced. If we set foot in the wards without invitation, without permission, we shall be regarded as intruders, unwelcome ones at that. We must wait – we must!" Her mouth was firm, her voice resolute, but there was a haunted look in her eyes. She was convinced of the rightness of her own actions and yet the necessity for it tore at her heart. Carrie had turned away, sickened. Out there men lay dying, suffering untold miseries. Perhaps Jamie was amongst them. Her heart twisted in panic and silently she prayed. 'Don't let him be out there. I want to find him, but not this way, not *here*!"

The days passed and the nurses grew resentful. Whilst they continued to sort linen, to mend and darn and count provisions, they could hear the screams and cries of the wounded and sick. Miss Nightingale remained tight-lipped and resolute. And the nurses began to think she did not care. Only Carrie understood the reasons for her actions, and yet even she began to think Miss Nightingale was wrong.

"The only thing we're allowed to do is cook extra food in our own kitchen," grumbled one of the nurses, "and then only if a doctor has requested it."

"Why aren't we allowed near the patients?" asked Ellen, a scullery-maid who had been dismissed from her last employment without a reference for having a follower. "Don't they trust us?" She grinned at Carrie cheekily, the suggestion in her tone implying that her ministrations to the soldiers' comforts might exceed those rules set by Miss Nightingale.

"I'm sure Miss Nightingale knows best," Carrie said, bending her head over her sewing of an arm-sling to hide the anger shining in her own eyes.

Less than an hour later she was bending over the rickety table Miss Nightingale used as a desk, repeating the very same question the young girl had asked. "Why aren't we allowed near the patients? We can hear them – dying in agony! We can smell the stench of death. The conditions out there," she waved her hand towards the part of the building which housed the wards, "must be intolerable. If we have lice and rats in our quarters – and we have – what on earth must it be like in there? You've seen it. You've toured the wards, haven't you? Well? You can't tell me we're not needed – desperately – by those men?"

Miss Nightingale's grey eyes regarded Carrie steadily, silently reproaching her for her display of temper.

"I'm sorry," Carrie said swiftly, even, before Miss Nightingale had uttered a word. "But – but, oh it seems so pointless our being here if we are allowed to do nothing – absolutely *nothing*!"

"We shall be – soon. I'm sure," Miss Nightingale said quietly, but with conviction. "We must wait until we are asked."

And that was all she would say.

It seemed to the impatient nurses a long time that they waited in idleness whilst only yards away men died for want of attention, but in fact it was only a few days, for on the 9th of November, four days after their arrival, there came such an influx of sick and wounded following the Battle of Inkerman, that in desperation the doctors and officials turned to Miss Nightingale and her nurses for help.

"At last," she told her nurses, her grey eyes alight with the fire of the challenge, "we have been asked for help. We can begin our work . . ."

At once excited chatter broke out amongst the women, but Miss Nightingale held up her hands. "I must ask you to remember – at all times – that we are under orders from the doctors. No one – not one of you – is to undertake to do anything without a direct order from me or from a doctor. Neither must you give commands to the ward orderlies. We shall find much to be done, you will work until you want to drop, and even then you will carry on, but you will work quietly and efficiently and – submissively. Do I make myself clear?

"Very well, then. Now, the first task is bedding. Many of the men have no beds to lie on, so we must make some straw palliasses . . ."

So their work began. The wards were overflowing so that men lay in the corridors on the stuffed sacks, with just enough room to pass between them. Then the bags of straw were all used up and the men lay on the bare boards. The floors were filthy and verminous and the men'no better. They were surprised to see the band of women moving quietly amongst them.

"I shouldn't come near me, lovey," one soldier, his face caked with mud, his hair and beard matted, said to Carrie. A filthy bandage wrapped his head and his left trouser leg was torn to the knee to reveal an open wound in his leg, the blood oozing from it on to the floor.

"Why ever not?" Carrie asked bending towards him. She could not kneel beside him, for the wooden floor was running with stinking liquid.

"I'm not fit for a lady to come near me."

Carrie laughed. "I'm no lady, I can tell you."

"By, you're from home!" The man's eyes brightened and for an instant the suffering, the pain, the filth, were forgotten as he was reminded of England. "I'd know that tongue anywhere, b'God. Aw lass, 'tis good to hear your voice!"

"*Now* will thou let me help?"

"Ay, an' I reckon I will, at that." Then he looked at the bundle of clothing in her arms. "That's not some clean clothes, is it?"

"It is. Now, let's be gettin' those off you and these on."

"Aw well now, I dunno, I mean . . ." Embarrassment spread across his face.

Carrie smiled. "What's this? A bashful soldier. I never thought I'd live to see the day!"

He grinned sheepishly and allowed her to help him, for he could not manage without her help.

"Where are you from?"

"Near York, miss. And you?"

"Now that you ask, I don't rightly know. Me Pa was a railway builder, so we moved about the country. We finished up near Manchester." She chattered on, asking him questions about his family, his home, anything to keep his mind off the job in hand – the changing of his clothes.

"There now, it wasn't so bad, was it?" she asked straightening up when they had finished.

"Nay, you'm a grand lass and no mistake."

"You – you don't happen to have heard of a Jamie Trent out here, do you?"

The soldier thought for a moment. "Nay, can't say I have. Why, he a relation of yourn?"

"Well, yes, My – my cousin. I – heard he was out here. I just wondered . . . Well, I must move on. I'll see you again."

The man lay back on the rough straw bed, but his eyes were fixed upon Carrie's slight figure as she moved amongst the other patients.

Carrie had thought her experiences, the harshness of her childhood, the years in India, had equipped her to face anything that life had to offer. But even she was appalled by the conditions at Scutari. She worked, as Miss Nightingale had predicted, until she wanted to drop, and then she still carried on working until fatigue enveloped her and she stole a few hours' exhausted sleep, to rise and begin again. It was worse, far worse than the cholera wards at the Middlesex Hospital. The sick and wounded poured in and of each one whom Carrie attended she asked the same question.

"Have you met anyone called James Trent out here?"

Day after day the answer was always no, and then one night she came upon a young boy of no more than sixteen or so who had been brought in that afternoon with a sabre wound in his chest. His breathing was rasping and obviously the boy was in great pain. Carrie washed him and made him as comfortable as she could. She was about to turn away, omitting to ask the boy her usual question, for obviously talking would exert him further, when he caught hold of her skirt. She turned back and bent down.

"What's – your – name?"

"Carrie Foster."

The boy smiled and closed his eyes, but his fingers still gripped her dress. Then his eyes fluttered open. "Carrie. That's funny. I got friendly with a chap in our camp. He talked about a girl back home called Carrie. Delirious, he was, with the cholera. He was callin' her name. When he got a bit better I asked 'im about her. But he wouldn't tell me nothing. Said it was all a long time ago."

Carrie's heart was thumping madly. "What – was your friend's name?" she whispered tensely, steeling herself against disappointment.

"Name? Oh yes, his name. James Trent, that was it."

The boy had fallen asleep and Carrie could ask no more questions. She stood up and moved away as if in a trance. Jamie was here! She had met someone who had known him.

Cholera! The boy had said Jamie had cholera. Carrie's heart contracted in fear. Very few men had cholera and survived. But then the boy had said Jamie had got better. No, no, what he had said was that when Jamie had got a *little* better, he'd asked him who Carrie was. He had not said that he'd recovered completely. Then, why wasn't he here in the hospital? She was sure he could not be here. Every evening, she followed Miss Nightingale and her lamp through the wards, searching, always searching for Jamie and yet dreading to see him lying in this hospital.

How could she find him, how could she search for him? She had come as a nurse, she had hidden the real motive for her desire to come to the Crimea from Miss Nightingale. How could she now desert Miss Nightingale and betray the trust she had placed in her? How could she deplete the number of nurses so badly needed by the men? True, another batch of women had arrived, much to Miss Nightingale's dismay, for she found difficulty in uniting the diverse members of the first party and forming them into a hard-working band, without doubling the number.

Hour after weary hour, Carrie washed and bathed and bandaged, scrubbed and cleaned, held the hand of dying men, comforting those about to face the butchery of the surgeon's knife and all the time her thoughts were filled with one name. 'Jamie, Jamie, how can I find you?'

Her opportunity came unexpectedly. When the hospital ships arrived from Balaclava, much to Miss Nightingale's horror they were often anchored in the Bosphorus for a week or so before the sick were landed.

"It's appalling," she told Carrie, in a rare moment of confiding in her. "The men tell me that the wounded are often on board ship for fourteen days or so before they even leave the Crimea, then they have the ghastly sea voyage across the Black Sea of four or five days and then to think that they lay out there," she waved her hand in disgust towards the sea, "before they are brought to us. Is it any wonder the death rate is so high?"

"What can we do?" Carrie asked.

"Very little, I'm afraid," replied Miss Nightingale caustically. She glanced down at a letter she held in her hand.

"I've received a note from a major aboard the ship now lying in the Bosphorus. He's not among the wounded, I understand. I'm not quite sure what he's doing aboard – some official business, no doubt. He says he has heard of our arrival and asks if I could send my very best nurse out with some supplies '*so that she may attend the sick and wounded, and lessen their suffering, I am sure.*' Will you go?" Miss Nightingale looked up at Carrie.

Carrie's heart leapt. Here was the chance she had been waiting for, to get away from the hospital, even if only for a short time. That way she might find out more positive news of Jamie.

"Of course," she breathed, scarcely able to hide the joy from showing in her eyes. "When do I leave?"

"Make up a first-aid kit from our stores. Take all you can manage. In fact, take one of the younger girls with you too. We can spare two of you, and it sounds as if your ministrations are badly needed out there."

"How – how long do we stay aboard?"

"You will leave at first light tomorrow and be away from the ship by dusk."

"Only one day, ma'am? That will scarce be time to attend to a quarter of the number on board."

"You may go back again the following day."

"Wouldn't it be more sensible to remain on board overnight?"

"It would – but think of the danger you would be placing yourself in."

"Among sick and starving men," Carrie said scathingly.

"The loss of your reputation . . ."

"Madam, if I ever had any such *reputation*, then it was lost many years ago," she added softly.

"Oh, well," Miss Nightingale sighed. "You had best use your own judgment, I suppose."

Carrie turned away to hide the light of triumph in her eyes.

"Oh I'll be seasick again, Mrs Foster," wailed Ellen, trudging after Carrie down the muddy track towards the landing-stage. "You knows how bad I was when we come."

"Nonsense, Ellen, the sea's as calm as a millpond, look at it."

Carrie soon found a caique to take them out to the ship lying at anchor in the Bosphorus, and despite Ellen's continuous wailing, they boarded the ship quite safely.

"The Lord save us!" Ellen cried, her mouth dropping open, her eyes wide as she gazed around the deck of the ship. Grim-faced and silent, Carrie's eyes, too, took in the dreadful aspect.

Men lay on the open deck, mostly with no bedding, not even a covering blanket. Their clothes were unrecognisable as the British uniform, so torn and tattered and filthy were they. Some had open wounds with no kind of dressing, others with dressings so dirty that they undoubtedly did more harm than good to the wound they covered.

"Good day, Mrs Foster." A voice spoke close behind her.

Carrie gasped and her whole being stiffened. Slowly she turned and looked up at the man standing behind her, a smile of satisfaction upon his face.

"Captain Richmond!" Her voice was a hoarse whisper.

"*Major* Richmond, ma'am, at your service." He bowed mockingly. "I had hoped my letter might bring you. I guessed that amongst Miss Nightingale's motley band . . ." he glanced meaningly at poor Ellen, "that you would stand out as a jewel amongst the rest."

"You – knew I was there?"

"Oh, yes," Major Richmond replied with confidence. "I have followed your every move, my dear, since you left India – in such haste!" His eyes glittered dangerously. Carrie swallowed the fear that rose in her throat. *He has not forgiven me for escaping from him,* she thought.

"But how – how do you come to be here – in the Crimea?"

Major Richmond tapped the side of his nose. "It pays to have relatives in high office, especially when one wants a transfer in a hurry." He laughed. "And I managed a promotion out of it too – though it cost me a pretty penny, I can tell you. Still . . ." His hand reached out and caressed the sleeve of her dress. "It was worth it for sight of you again. You see," his soft tone was full of menace. "I told you you could not escape me."

Carrie felt a shudder run through her as she shrank from his touch, but she would not let this man know the fear he brought to her heart. Defiantly, she tossed her head. "You will excuse me, Major, we have work to do aboard this ship."

"Of course, ma'am." He bowed again. "I will not detain you – *now*!"

He turned on his heel and walked swiftly away, passing through the lines of wounded men lying on the deck without even glancing down at them. Carrie stared after him. Ruthless as ever, she thought, and shivered again. It became even more imperative that she should find Jamie, for he was her only protection against Major Jeremy Richmond.

"Who is 'ee, Mrs Foster?" Ellen whispered. "How do you know him?"

"I had the misfortune to meet him in India," murmured Carrie wryly. "I had hoped never to meet with him again, but it seems . . . Come," she said, shaking herself, "we have work to do."

The following hours were taken up with the task of trying to make as many of the wounded and sick as comfortable as possible. Men with cholera and dysentery lay alongside those with wounds, so that very soon the wounded men had not only the pain of their injury to suffer, but the sickness too. They had lain on the bare decks, so that their backs were red raw. They were cold, filthy and starving.

"This is intolerable!" Carrie muttered angrily, straightening her aching back. She looked about her and then glanced towards the setting sun. Dark clouds were gathering with the threat of rain. It was obvious the men on deck would have no shelter.

"Where is Major Richmond?" she demanded of one of the crew.

The man shrugged uncaringly. " 'Ow should I know," then he grinned, showing blackened teeth. "But if you'm lookin' for a man, darlin', I'll . . ."

Carrie turned away, disgust upon her face. She glanced towards the bridge and her eyes met the gaze of the man she was obliged, out of necessity, to seek. She crossed the deck towards him, stopping now and then to help one of the injured. Major Richmond descended from the bridge and came towards her.

"Ah, your work finished for the day, my dear? Then will you come below to my cabin . . .?"

"Major Richmond, this work will *never* be finished," she began angrily. "Is there no shelter for these men? Look," she gestured towards the darkening sky. "It's going to rain soon. What are you going to do about it?"

"Ma'am, I am a man with power at my fingertips, but even my influence does not extend to the elements!"

"Don't treat me like a fool, Major," she snapped.

"Never that, ma'am, I assure you," he said sarcastically. "If you will permit me to give you a little refreshment after your labours," he held out his hand to her, "then we will discuss the matter."

"I don't think . . ."

The Major made as if to turn away, shrugging his shoulders, "Then there is no more to be said."

Carrie glanced back at the men lying on the deck. Then she felt the first drop of rain upon her cheek. In desperation she turned back to him. "Very well, then," she said resignedly, trying to ignore the triumph which leapt into his eyes.

Below decks, in his cabin, the Major had evidently anticipated her acceptance of his invitation, for the meal on the table was the nearest to a banquet which Carrie had seen since leaving England.

"How do you come to have all this," she gasped, "when the men out there are starving?"

"I told you I had power at my fingertips. Pray be seated, my dear."

"No," she said sharply, "I couldn't, not when . . ."

"My dear Carrie, this small meal would be as nothing to the number of men out there."

She whirled to face him. "How can you sit here gorging yourself, knowing your men are wounded, sick and starving?"

"There's no point in getting emotional about the situation. The officers in command must keep themselves fit and well, as must you, their nurse. Now, be sensible and eat."

"No," Carrie replied defiantly.

Major Richmond gave an exaggerated sigh. "Still as stubborn, I see. Still determined to play the heroine as you were in that campful of cholera-ridden natives."

"What are you going to do about those men on deck?"

"Absolutely nothing, my dear." Major Richmond seated himself at the table and spread his napkin across his knee. "If you will not join me, then there is nothing further to discuss."

For a moment Carrie stood irresolute, staring at him in disbelief. She had recognised him for a hard, ruthless man who would do anything to get his own way, but she had not thought that even he would stoop as low as this – to neglect his soldiers' well-being, to use them as pawns to blackmail her into submission! His passion for her – for it could not be called love – must be far greater than she had imagined. He had carried out his threat to follow her from India, to follow her wherever she went in the world. 'You will not escape me', he had promised, and now that promise – or, rather, threat – had been fulfilled. As she watched him begin to eat, her loathing for him overflowed. Then she remembered the men on deck, the encroaching darkness, the threatening storm.

Reluctantly she sat down opposite him. He grinned at her. "It's really very good, my dear, do try some."

Sick with revulsion she picked at the food upon her plate, merely to satisfy this man's whim. She must get him to do something for those men up there.

"Major Richmond, please . . ."

"Ah, now that is more the tone of voice I like to hear from you." He reached out and touched her cheek. Though she cringed inwardly,

Carrie clenched her teeth and restrained herself from slapping his hand away.

"Please – will you do something for those men?"

"Ah, yes, the men." He raised his voice. "Sergeant."

The cabin door flew open. There was a stamping of feet as the man came to attention with a sharp "Sir!"

"Arrange for the wounded on deck to be taken ashore. See what covering or shelter you can afford for those waiting."

"Y-yes, sir," the man's surprise was evident. "Right away, sir."

The door closed behind him.

"You see," Major Richmond said smilingly, "what it means to have power? I usually get my own way in the end, you know."

Not in everything, thought Carrie determinedly.

"Do have some wine, my dear, I'm sure you'll find it to your liking."

Major Richmond seemed determined to savour every mouthful of his meal and every sip of his wine. The minutes lengthened into hours and Carrie, weary, not only from this day's work, but from the weeks of hard, grinding labour, found her limbs grow heavy and her eyes drowsy from the warmth of the cabin, the headiness of the wine, the comfort of the chair.

She was unaware of the Major lifting her on to a couch, of him covering her with a blanket and then stealthily leaving the cabin.

When Carrie awoke, at first she did not realise where she was. It was so blissfully comfortable, so warm, so restful. Her aching body luxuriated in the soothing softness of the couch. She became aware of a gentle rocking motion and as wakefulness came, she looked about her. The remains of the Major's dinner still lay on the table, though light streamed in through the porthole. Bright light! Daylight!

Carrie was fully awake in a moment. She must have slept the night through. She sat up and swung her legs to the floor and stood up. Smoothing her crumpled dress and ruffled hair, she went to the door of the cabin. Twisting the knob she found she could not open the door. It was locked!

Stunned for a moment she could not think properly. Then she

became aware that the ship's motion was far greater than the previous day when they had been at anchor.

She went to the porthole.

They were moving. The ship was out at sea, the shore a speck in the distance.

"Oh, no, no," Carrie cried and covered her face with her hands. How could she have been so foolish?

He had planned this. From the beginning, from the moment he had sent that letter to Miss Nightingale – perhaps even long before that for all she knew – he had planned this abduction.

Anger flooded through her. What of the wounded? Then she remembered. He had given the order last evening for the wounded to be ferried ashore. No doubt this had gone on all night whilst she slept in a locked cabin, and now with the morning they were out into the Black Sea.

"Jamie, oh, Jamie. I need you so much!" She closed her eyes.

During the previous day she had had little time to ask her usual question of the men on board and whilst she had attended to many she had not seen all of them. Ellen had descended to the lower decks to tend the men below.

The situation held more irony than Carrie knew.

At the moment when she awoke to find herself a virtual prisoner aboard the ship and sailing back across the Black Sea towards the Crimea, the wounded were being carried up the steep slope to the Barrack Hospital. Amongst them was a soldier with his arm badly smashed by a musket ball. Like his companions he was more dead than alive, dirty, half-starved, unshaven and cold.

His name was Corporal James Trent!

Chapter Nine

James Trent lay on sacking on the floor of the Barrack Hospital. He was slipping towards death. His eyes were closed against the sight of his companions and their suffering, but he could not shut out the sound of their moans, or the shrill cries as they were carried towards the small room where the doctors now operated instead of on the floor of the ward in full view of all the patients.

Perhaps he would lose his arm. Not that he really cared. How he had survived until now he didn't know – but it could not be for much longer. He was luckier than the many who had lain in that place before him, for now – slowly but surely – Miss Nightingale's influence was beginning to take effect. The floors were clean, the beds reasonably so. There was clean clothing and food.

Jamie Trent had a chance of survival – if he had the will to take it.

He was by no means a coward, but it was so like the time in Abbeyford – what was it now, thirteen years ago, or more? There had been nothing left worth fighting for, not after he had lost Carrie, after he had watched her ride away from him for ever, as another man's wife. How he had loved her wild, gypsy beauty, her bright violet eyes, her black, flying hair. He had loved her strength, her passionate nature – even her jealousy when she had spied on him talking to Francesca. How angry she had been. And then that anger had turned to love in a moment and they had become as one.

Jamie smiled faintly as he remembered and the pain lessened a little. His memories of her were still so vivid. She was part of him. He would never be free of his love for her.

How many times during the years since had he gone over and over the events in his mind and wished his own actions so very different. If only – he had not ridden away in a moment of senseless, wild anger, ignoring Carrie's desperate cries. If only – he had not entrusted his letter to her brother. If only – he hadn't galloped like a mad thing on a pointless journey to the lawyers in Manchester. If only – if only – if only ...

Someone was bending over him, shaking his arm gently, trying to arouse him. "Sir! Sir! Corporal Trent. It's me – Boy. Don't you remember?" No one knew Boy's real name. Not even he knew it, for he had been an orphan living on the streets of London until at the earliest possible moment he had taken the Queen's shilling and joined Her Majesty's army.

He was a wiry little fellow, unaccountably cheerful and willing. The name officially given him was 'John Smith' but he had become known as 'Boy' to men and officers alike.

Jamie was drifting, slipping into a world of memories, dreaming of Carrie and he did not want to be aroused back to the pain and suffering. He just wanted to drift away ... away ... But the voice was insistent, it would not let him go.

"Sir – I've got some'at to tell you. Do wake up, sir. *Please*!"

The pain was throbbing in his arm again, the noises of those nearby were pressing upon him once more. Jamie sighed and grimaced, shifted his sore and aching back a little and opened his eyes. "Hello, Boy," he said flatly. "You here too?"

"Aye, bin here abit, I 'ave. Gettin' better, I am now, sir, thanks to these nurses. Eh, that's what I want to tell you, sir."

Jamie's eyes were beginning to close again. "Sir!" The tone was reproachful. "Do listen, sir. I reckon it's important."

"Go on, then," Jamie said resignedly, his eyes still shut. "I'm listening."

"Well, sir, you know when you had that bout of cholera, an' I helped look after you, you was on about a girl called Carrie."

"Mmmm?"

"Well, she's here," Boy said triumphantly. "She's one of Miss Nightingale's nurses!"

Jamie's eyes flew open in an instant. "Here? She can't be – she ... Boy – are you sure?"

Boy nodded gleefully. "She was asking about you. She's been asking everybody who's come here nearly – so I've heard – an' it was me who knew you." He was so proud to be involved.

"Where is she?"

Boy's face fell a little. "That's the only trouble. Since you've been here these last three days, I ain't seen her. I've been burstin' to tell 'er, and I can't find 'er nowhere. An' you've bin lyin' here half dead since you come." He sniffed in a matter-of-fact manner. "I was afraid you was goin' to snuff it 'afore I could tell you."

Die! Oh, hell! Jamie thought, not now! I'll not die now. Only moments before he'd been close to it, allowing himself to slip over the edge into blissful oblivion. But not now, not any more if Carrie were here. If she was somewhere close again, if he could just see her!

His hand reached out and clasped Boy's arm, trying to raise himself up. "Boy – who d'you say is in charge of the nurses?"

"Miss Nightingale."

"I must see her."

"She comes round at night – goes all over the hospital, carrying one of those Turkish lamp things. It's dusk now. She'll be along soon."

Jamie sank back again. "You're sure Carrie's here? She's not gone away again?"

"I dunno. I can't find anyone who seems to know." He paused. "Except Ellen. When I asked her she wouldn't seem to answer me proper. Looked upset, I thought ... Oh God," he glanced down at Jamie the words spilling out before he thought to check them. "I hope she ain't ill. Some of the nurses get cholera."

Jamie groaned aloud, whilst Boy watched him, biting his lips anxiously. He stayed with Jamie, squatting on the floor beside him, watching the long corridor for the pale, flickering light which would herald Miss Nightingale's approach.

"She's here – she's coming!" Again he was shaking Jamie into wakefulness.

"What? Who? Carrie?" Jamie tried to pull himself up.

"No. Miss Nightingale." Boy began to scramble up.

"Miss Nightingale – Miss Nightingale," he said in a loud whisper. "Please, ma'am, would you step over here a moment. Corporal Trent wants to speak with you urgent."

Jamie saw the tall woman stop, hold her lamp high and look across in his direction. The light moved nearer and she was standing beside him.

"How may I help you?" Her voice was soft and reassuring, yet firm and confident.

"I'll get you a camp-stool." Boy fetched one and returned to place it beside where Jamie lay. Miss Nightingale set her lamp upon the floor and sat down. "Well?"

"Ma'am, have you a Carrie Smithson – no – no, wait a minute – a Mrs Carrie Foster here as one of your nurses?"

There was a moment's pause, but Miss Nightingale's face showed no change of expression. "May I ask why you want to know?"

For a moment Jamie closed his eyes, unable to answer. Why, she asked. If only she *knew*!"

"You must understand, Corporal Trent," her voice was gentle yet there was authority there. "That I must exert a strict discipline over my nurses, and ..."

"Yes, yes, of course. I appreciate that, ma'am," he assured her hastily, "and I can promise you I do not in any way wish to cause you any trouble or embarrassment, only – I – beg you – let me see her – just let me speak to her."

He was silent, the words would not come. He could not explain to this quiet, composed woman all the craving in his heart which had been locked away there for thirteen lonely years. Would she – could she even – understand? Did she know what it was to love? Had she ever loved and lost, and then been given the chance of finding her beloved again?

Boy, hovering near, was bending forward, whispering to her. "He loved her, ma'am, a long while back – only they was parted, I reckon. He won't say much, but – if you could help him, ma'am, I reckon she's all he's got to live for – if you sees what I mean."

Her gaze was upon Jamie's gaunt face, accentuated by the pale lamplight. "She is one of my nurses – yes," Miss Nightingale said slowly, "but I'm afraid she's not here at present."

"Why? Is she ill?" Jamie asked, afraid of the answer.

"I – trust not. I was asked to send a nurse aboard the ship you arrived on whilst it lay at anchor off Scutari. I sent Mrs Foster and a young girl, Ellen, with her." Miss Nightingale sighed. "Ellen returned with the wounded when they were brought ashore – but not Mrs Foster."

"What happened to her? Did the girl say nothing?"

"I have questioned Ellen closely and it seems there was a major on board – she didn't know his name, though I've since learnt from the soldiers his name was Richmond – the same man who wrote the letter to me asking me for my help. Evidently he had met Mrs Foster in India."

"India?" Jamie's surprise was evident.

"She had been in India with her husband – did you not know?"

"I – knew she was married," his eyes were filled with pain, "but not where they had gone."

"Her husband was killed in India. Didn't you know that either?"

"No. No, I didn't."

There was a pause whilst Jamie took in this information and all its implications. He raised his worried eyes again to Miss Nightingale's calm face. "But what can have happened on board the ship? Who was this – this Major Richmond?"

There was bleak misery in his eyes, which Miss Nightingale could not fail to see even in the dim, fitful light. Had he found Carrie only to lose her again?

"If it's any comfort to you," she said gently. "Mrs Foster did not seem at all pleased to see the Major – in fact, Ellen says she seemed afraid of him."

"Carrie – afraid?" Jamie almost smiled at the thought of his wild gypsy love being afraid of anyone. But that had been thirteen long years ago. He knew nothing of her life since with her husband, in a strange land. His expression was haunted.

"Ellen last saw her arguing with this Major about shelter for the wounded from an approaching storm."

Jamie nodded. "Yes – I remember. It rained like hell when we were being brought ashore. I beg your pardon, ma'am," he apologised swiftly, "army life has robbed me of my manners."

Miss Nightingale nodded slightly and said, "Corporal Trent, you do wish to know *everything* I know?"

"Why, yes, of course. There's – more?"

She sighed. "Yes. And it may be distasteful to you to hear it. Ellen heard the Major refuse to discuss helping the wounded unless Mrs Foster went below with him."

"And?" His face was dark now with anguish.

She lifted her shoulders fractionally, almost sadly. "She went."

He groaned, unable to stop the sound escaping from his lips.

After a few moments Jamie said quietly. "They began taking us ashore and even tried to rig up some improvised shelter for those waiting on deck. Whatever happened, she evidently succeeded in persuading the Major to help the wounded." There was bitter sarcasm in his tone as his imagination played cruel tricks on him, forcing him to picture her in the unknown Major's arms in exchange for the well-being of the wounded.

"Has the ship sailed back to the Crimea yet?"

"Yes, it left as soon as all the wounded had been put ashore."

"To think she was on that boat – and I didn't even know," he murmured. "If only . . ."

"I'm sorry – truly," Miss Nightingale said with compassion.

Then, as if filled with a new purpose, Jamie said, "My arm? How bad is my injury?"

"The doctor thinks it may have to be amputated. Tomorrow he . . ."

"No. Leave it. I will not be operated on. It'll heal. It'll have to. I'll be out of here. I must go in search of her. I won't lose her a second time!"

"Corporal Trent." The firmness was now more in evidence. "You will, whilst you are my patient, do what is best for your recovery." Then her tone softened. "For the present – concentrate on your own health – I will do what I can to help you in – the other matter."

Then she was gone, moving amongst the other patients, giving a drink to one, covering another and holding the hand of a dying man.

Jamie lay back. The pain was back in his arm with a vengeance but now he didn't care. Now he had something to live for – he had to find Carrie again!

Now there was a future for them together.

"What is the meaning of this?" Carrie demanded of her captor when finally the door of the cabin opened and Major Richmond entered.

"I should have thought that was quite clear, Carrie my love," he drawled. "I have no intention of allowing you to escape from me again. As soon as we get to my quarters, I shall arrange for the chaplain to marry us!"

"Never, never!" Carrie screamed at him.

"Oh, I think you will agree, my dear," he said menacingly, moving closer to her. He reached out and pulled her towards him, pressing his mouth upon hers. Carrie struggled, but his arms were strong about her, his body trapping her against the wooden wall of the cabin. She fought and clawed her way free until they stood back from each other panting, the one from exertion the other from frustrated passion.

"You *will* agree to marry me," he gasped, his eyes dark with hunger for her.

Carrie shook her head. "No – I'd rather *die* first!"

His laugh was humourless. "You probably will do, my dear, if you refuse my protection." He moved closer again. "Not all our soldiers are weak and ill. Whilst they may not enjoy the best of health or conditions, they are strong and lusty." He paused a moment to let his words sink in. "A beautiful young woman alone amongst a herd of men who have not held a woman for months . . ."

"You are *despicable*," Carrie spat at him, but the Major only laughed.

Carrie remained a prisoner in his cabin for the five days the voyage took. Not that she wanted for anything. Food was plentiful and even fresh clothing was provided – a velvet gown and a black velvet cloak. But his outward show of generosity only confirmed for Carrie the thought that he had planned all this so carefully in advance.

The ship docked at Balaclava and Carrie found herself conducted to a house not far from the dock area, and there the Major left her.

At once Carrie tried to escape, but immediately found that not only had the so-called housekeeper – a slattern of a woman, dirty and fat – been instructed to keep watch on her, but two soldiers had been posted outside the door.

Carrie sat in the room and tried to compose her emotions, tried to remain calm and rational, to plan her escape sensibly. But every moment that passed brought her nearer to the time the Major would return with the army chaplain. She could not bribe the woman and the two soldiers, for she had no money.

She heard footsteps on the stairs and felt her flesh creep as she knew he was returning. Major Richmond was alone but in a vile temper. He banged the door behind him.

"There's not a chaplain to be found. All up near the front line, performing their *admirable* duties," he said sarcastically. Carrie breathed a sigh of relief and some of that relief must have shown on her face, for Major Richmond pointed his finger at her. "Don't look so pleased with yourself, madam. I'm not finished yet!" He stepped towards her and grasped her shoulders. "But what need have we of a parson, my lovely. I've waited long enough to taste your sweetness for myself. You've taunted me long enough, held me at arm's length when your husband was alive to protect you. Escaped me after he died. But now there's no one here – no one to help you. Not even your precious James Trent!"

He felt her go rigid beneath his grasp, her eyes widen, her lips part. "Jamie – you know where he is?"

His anger grew. He shook her fiercely. "Why can't it be me? Why, at the very mention of his name, do you look like that?" He was almost weeping with frustration. Then he flung her from him so that she fell to the floor whilst he stood over her. "Yes – I know where he is. He was shot in the arm. Badly wounded." He leant over her, menacing, gleeful. "*Fatally* wounded. He's dead, your hero, your beloved. Dead, do you hear me?" His voice rose to a high pitch. He raised his hand to strike her, but his words, his venomous anger galvanised her into action. With the inborn tenacity for survival, she sprang to her feet and flung herself at him, her fists and feet flailing. Surprised by her sudden retaliation, he fell backwards, but Carrie did not wait to see what happened, for she wrenched open the door and fled. Down the stairs, out of the house, she began to run wildly without thought for direction or purpose. She must just escape from him.

The two soldiers had relaxed their vigil now that Major Richmond had returned. In fact they were in the housekeeper's kitchen, flirting with the woman and drinking.

Carrie ran on. Fortunately, her flight was in the right direction and within moments she saw ahead of her the mast of the ship she had so recently left still anchored near the dock. She glanced fearfully behind her, but there was no one in pursuit. Not yet.

Her heart was pounding, her breathing laboured, but on she ran, her legs weak and shaking. As she neared the landing-stage she saw that more wounded were being carried aboard the ship. Thankfully she threaded her way amongst them, glancing behind her every now and then. She reached the gangway and was obliged to pause whilst the stretcher-bearers carried their sick and wounded on board. She waited, panting heavily, almost sick with fear. She began to climb aboard and was halfway up the gangway when she saw Major Richmond running towards the landing-stage, followed by the two soldiers.

"Oh, please let me pass. I am a nurse. Please let me reach the Captain."

" 'Ere, who are you pushing?" snapped one stretcher-bearer. At that moment the burly figure of the Captain of the ship appeared at the top of the gangway.

"Let her through," he bellowed. "She's one of Miss Nightingale's nurses." Then he pointed to the running men below, to the Major and his two followers. "And stop those men coming aboard!"

Five or six of his own crew plunged down the gangplank and with bloodcurdling yells they rushed towards the Major and his men. She saw Jeremy Richmond stop and hesitate. Then he glanced up at Carrie, who had now reached the top of the gangway and was standing close beside the burly, protective figure of the Captain.

He shook his fist but once, and then, as the sailors drew nearer, both he and the two soldiers turned and ran.

Relief flooded through Carrie so that her legs gave way. She felt the strong arm of the Captain about her waist, but it was only offered as a comfort, a support.

"Let me help you, ma'am," he said politely.

"Oh, Captain, how can I ever thank you? You don't know how much you've helped me."

"I think I do, ma'am," the big man said quietly.

"You – you do?" Carrie was surprised. As the Captain led her below to the comfort of the cabin she had so recently vacated, though this time no longer any man's prisoner, he explained. "I watched you, ma'am, all that first day, tending they poor fellows, the wounded soldiers I have to bring by the thousand." He shook his head. "Ma'am, it fair breaks my heart to see it and I'm given no help to tend them, no help at all. I was right glad to see you come aboard, ma'am. Then I thought it strange that the Major ordered them put ashore in the dark of night, but I made no argument, seein' as how it was gettin' them to hospital the quicker. Then, when they was all ashore, he starts chafin' me to go about and start back for the Crimea. Well," he shrugged his huge shoulders, "I had no reason to linger, and the conditions bein' right, I did as he bid. It wasn't until we was a day at sea that I learnt you was still aboard. I swear that's the truth, ma'am. I had no part in his plan."

"I believe you, Captain," Carrie said softly. His actions a few moments ago had told her this fact.

"I thought there'd been a genuine mistake, that you'd fallen asleep after all the long hours you'd worked. You deserved some rest, if you don't mind my sayin' so, ma'am."

Carrie smiled.

"I said to him, 'Shall I put back to Scutari, Major, and take the young lady ashore?' 'No, my man, you will not,' ses he in that haughty way of his. 'There's been no mistake, I assure you'. Well, I didn't know what to think. An' then a member of my crew said the cabin door was locked, an' I didn't know whether you'd locked it against intruders or what was goin' on. Then when we docked at Balaclava and he hustled you ashore, I could see you wasn't goin' willingly, so as soon as I saw you runnin' towards the ship just now, I knew you needed my help real bad."

"Captain, I can't thank you enough!"

"Well, ma'am, it'll be a week or more till we can sail back to Scutari. I have me orders – not," he bent forward in a confidential whisper, "that I always agrees with them, but there it is. I'm not allowed to sail till I have a shipload of wounded and sick, so I can't see but that you'll have to stay aboard. But I'll see you come to no harm, ma'am, I promise you that. You and that there Miss Nightingale are doin' a fine job, and you have my admiration."

"Thank you, Captain. I shall be only too glad to stay on board. In the meantime, until we sail, I shall do whatever I can to help the wounded."

The Captain, bearded and burly, patted her shoulder with his huge hand in a fatherly gesture. "Good, good, and I will do what I can to obtain some medical supplies for you, if you promise not to ask *how* I obtained them!" He tapped the side of his nose and winked broadly.

Carrie laughed. "Oh, I promise you that, Captain."

The big man laughed heartily and left the cabin. Carrie sank on to the couch, listening to his laughter still resounding as he returned on deck.

It was only then that the full realisation of Major Richmond's words hit her.

"Jamie Trent is dead!"

With a deep moan, Carrie flung herself face downwards on the couch and gave way to an uncharacteristic storm of weeping.

The emotional storm passed but left her feeling exhausted and drained. She bathed her face and went on deck resolved to bury her own misery in hard work helping the wounded. But her whole world had disintegrated with the Major's words. 'Jamie Trent is dead'. Her very reason for living was gone. The thought of finding him again one day had kept her going through all the sorrow of parting, through the long years of a loveless marriage. And now, when she had followed him half way round the world, to find that he was dead was almost more than she could bear.

But her fighting instincts, her will to survive, would not let her give in, even yet. Instead she threw herself into her work, scarcely noticing whether she ate, or washed, or slept, whether it was day or night. She was only aware of the dull ache in her own heart and of the men in her care. Still she managed to smile, to comfort, to bathe and bandage, whilst all the time her heart was breaking.

On the day following his conversation with Miss Nightingale, the surgeon chopped off Jamie's left arm and with it all his hopes for a future with Carrie.

Physically he recovered, but emotionally he was plunged once more into the bottomless pit of despair. For a time he lived in a crazy half-world somewhere between dreams of past happiness and the nightmare of the present. At last the only thought left in his now fully conscious mind was the torment of the decision he must make.

He opened his eyes to find Miss Nightingale bending over him. "Are you feeling a little stronger, Corporal Trent?"

His sigh was long and deep, almost as if he wished it could be his last breath. His voice was hoarse and expressionless. "Miss

Nightingale, I no longer wish to see Mrs Foster. In fact, I'd be obliged to you – should she return here – if you . . ." he paused hardly able to force the final disastrous words through his unwilling lips. "If you – could keep my presence here from her."

Miss Nightingale was thoughtful for a moment. "I understand the reason for your decision, but I think you are wrong. However," she straightened up, "that is not my concern. I may tell you that, should Mrs Foster return here, I shall be obliged to send her home to England – in the interests of discipline. So – she will not be on these wards again."

Jamie closed his eyes. It was the right decision. She would be better with her Major – a whole man. He was sure it was the right decision.

But, oh, how it finally shattered his already broken spirit!

Chapter Ten

London offered little hospitality for its wounded heroes. The meagre temporary pension Jamie was granted of sixpence per day could not buy lodgings, food and clothing – and it could be stopped at any time! Day after day he trudged the streets but no one wanted to employ a one-armed war casualty. At night he joined the tramps and vagrants along the Embankment and was embittered to see many of his companions were old soldiers.

But what shocked him even more was that they were not the only homeless. There were whole families, women and children huddled together in almost every available corner on the Embankment and in every recess across London Bridge!

Unable to sleep for the cold and the bitter misery in his heart, he stared at the dark shadows of the Thames. Beneath its cold waters he could seek oblivion. But then the remembered picture of his own grandfather dangling purple-faced, eyes and tongue bulging, from the stable rafters made him turn away from such a course with a shudder of revulsion. Suicide was not the answer.

Abbeyford! The name crept unbidden into his mind and memories stirred. That was were he belonged. The Manor was still his. At least it would be a shelter of sorts. Restlessly he moved his cramped and frozen feet.

Abbeyford! The place called him, set him yearning to be among the familiar fields and lanes. And there he could relive memories of the time shared with Carrie.

His mutilated body and his tattered emotions sought the only haven of happiness he had ever known.

Abbeyford! He would go back to Abbeyford.

As the train pulled away from Abbeyford Halt and the smoke drifted away, Jamie Trent looked about him. Grimly, he saw how the railway line tore through the very heart of the valley, an ugly scar across the green fields and quiet country lanes. His eyes, somewhat reluctantly, were drawn towards the Manor House. From this distance it looked surprisingly unaltered.

Without realising he had consciously moved, he found himself walking along the platform, through the white-painted gate – already hanging off its hinges – and down towards the village.

Two women passed him, staring at him and then whispering together as they went on. A man was limping towards him, his left leg swinging stiffly at each step so that he moved along with a rolling gait. He stopped a few feet in front of Jamie and stared at him. Jamie continued walking.

"Why, 'tis Master Jamie!" The man's face was altered in an instant from lines of fatigue by the grin which stretched his mouth. "Eh, Master Jamie! I'm glad to see you – we thought you was dead."

His glance fell upon the empty sleeve of Jamie's coat, and the grin faded. He gave a quick nod towards it. "You've bin hurt bad, I see. I'm sorry, Master Jamie."

"Thank you, Joby," Jamie said quietly. He had recognised Joby Greenfield at once, though the limp was something new. In turn, Jamie nodded towards Joby's left leg. "You too?"

"Aw, that's a legacy from that there fight we 'ad years back wi' t'railway navvies."

"How – how are things here now, Joby?"

Joby Greenfield shrugged with the philosophical acceptance of a man born to expect hardship. "Could be worse. A lot of the villagers have gone. Moved to towns to find work in t'factories." He paused, seeming to want to ask a question and yet not knowing quite how to phrase it. "You – you back for good, Master Jamie?"

Jamie's smile was a little thin, his eyes still mirroring the heavy weight of sadness in his heart. "I expect so, Joby. I've nowhere else to go."

He moved on again with a casual word of farewell. "Be seeing you again, Joby."

Jamie did not look back and so did not see the grin widening upon Joby's face as he watched him walk up the village street and take the lane towards the Manor House.

"Good to have you back, Master Jamie," he called after him, and Jamie waved his one hand in acknowledgement without turning round.

"Aye," Joby Greenfield murmured to himself. "You'm home now, m'lad, an' I reckon you'll be stayin' when you find out who's up at t'Manor!"

Jamie paused, his hand on the sagging gate-post leading into the stableyard from the lane. The gate was off its hinges, lying in the grass a few feet away. His eyes roamed over the stableyard, at the weeds pushing their way up between the cobblestones; the buildings, the timber rotting and some of the brickwork beginning to crumble. Slowly he moved across the yard and, avoiding the back entrance, he walked round the side of the house to the terrace.

The long windows stood open to the sunshine, the floor-length curtains billowed softly in the light breeze. Jamie stepped over the threshold and stopped in surprise.

The room was freshly decorated – the old chairs and sofas had been dust-beaten to a respectable condition. The carpet – worn and faded – had at least been scrubbed to cleanliness and the oak floor shone with polishing that must have taken a week!

Someone lived here. In his home!

He moved across the room and opened the door into the hall. It was still dimly lit, but no longer dismal. There was not a cobweb nor a dirty footprint to be seen.

Jamie sniffed. Was it possible? Baking bread? The smell drew him towards the kitchens. Now he could hear a woman humming softly to herself and the sounds of dough being slapped and kneaded. Quietly, he pushed open the door.

She was standing at the bare, scrubbed table, her hands busy with the dough, her slim body enveloped in a huge white apron.

A white scarf tied back her black, curling hair and a smudge of flour lay upon her cheek.

For a moment he thought – man though he was – that he was going to faint.

He whispered her name. "*Carrie!*"

She was suddenly still as if turned to stone. Then slowly, as if almost afraid it would not be true, she turned her violet eyes upon him.

He wasn't conscious of having moved towards her, but the next instant she was reaching up to touch his face, leaving traces of flour upon his cheeks too.

Wonderingly, her hands passed over his face, his chest, his waist, unable to believe he was real, whilst he stood drinking in the sight of her.

"I – thought you were – dead!" she breathed and then with a sigh of thankfulness she laid her head against his chest and wound her arms tightly around his waist. "What kept you away from me so long?" she murmured.

Jamie shook his head but could not speak. The time for explanations was later. Without asking, he knew why she had come back here. Back to Abbeyford. All roads led back to Abbeyford.

Now his mouth was hungry for the taste of her lips. His one arm held her close and they clung together, swaying slightly, lost in the ecstasy of their reunion.

He had come home – and so had she. Home to Abbeyford, home to happiness and to the hope of a new tomorrow.

And the ghosts of unhappy lovers past finally found their long-sought peace.

It had begun in Abbeyford and it ended in Abbeyford. And yet, it was not really the end, rather a new beginning.

Lightning Source UK Ltd.
Milton Keynes UK
UKOW04f2254241114

242079UK00003BA/68/P